THE BROTHERHOOD
OF LOST SOULS

Vol. 1: Prodigy of the Menace

For My Siblings

Jesusica

Daniela

Daniel

James

Justin

Liliana

Emily

Rachel

Contents

Reflection···3

The paths we choose···28

Hardship & Friendship···54

We need each other···85

Fight Night···114

Welcome to the Family···142

Familiar Faces···170

Cause & Effect   ···194

Consequences··· 222

Reflection

Silence accompanied my vengeance for a brief moment of unadulterated euphoria. After the sensation of final retribution had passed, I briefly considered the penance for murder. The man I had slain laid inches away staining the pavement of a small parking lot in the heart of the city. His face was unrecognizable, (though to his credit, neither was mine.) we waged war together. He deserved his fate & hell will greet him with open arms. Sirens began to echo in the distance. I knew they were for me, but I didn't want to run. I was ready to take accountability for my actions. My intention was met this very day.

A cigarette sounded good to calm my nerves, I didn't smoke, but it was as good a time as any. I had to bum one from the body next to me, he wasn't going to need them anyways. Just moments ago he was trying to kill me, the least he can do is donate a square to a good cause. I reached for his pack of cigarettes that peaked out of his far jacket pocket. He jolted like a possum in the road, so I sprang back startled and instinctively struck him. He scared the hell out of me to be honest, I almost screamed. Maybe he was dead and just blew out his remaining energy before the last punch, which is what I'd like to think. Either way he was dead for sure after that last blow. So I proceeded to grab his pack of cigarettes and lit one. Ugh, menthol too, this guy had poor taste in most things.

A crowd started to form (like I wasn't covered in blood next to a dead guy), guess they saw strength in numbers or something. They were ballsy as hell, one of the spectators actually testified against me. He thought I beat a guy to death over half a pack of cigarettes, finally getting my smokes back in the end. What an idiot, I'll admit I haven't exactly been an upstanding member of society but c'mon. This guy had no idea of what really went down, but then again, not many do. This was not personal, (well it was but not intentionally.) it was simply retaliation of the strongest form. He pushed me this far, it was either him or me, one of us had to go. As I look back on this moment there are no regrets still. Just relief that he will never hurt anyone again.

It felt like an eternity waiting for the police to arrive, I undoubtedly could have escaped, easily. Cops don't always rush to the scene of a crime when gang members are involved. Had I ran this would be another story. There was still a piece of my conscious left telling me to fess up. Normally my moral compass is a bit askew from most, I would run from the cops, if they were after me in another scenario. I'd gladly make the five o'clock news in a high-speed chase, or social up rise. Taking a life on the other hand was different, even if it was justified I couldn't flee, this was a first for me. I was not always like this, I used to be normal, living happily alongside the rest of society. White picket fence and all, when my family was whole. Back when the world was still beautiful in my eyes.

My mother was a second generation immigrant. Her father came over from Ireland when he was a teenager, working the fields to support his family. My mother had no accent growing up in the states, but she was Irish through and though. She even named my sister after her Irish father, Christy. My mother was named after her grandmother Alice, it was almost tradition to honor a family member though children. She died giving birth to my little sister when I was just a boy, but we kept her alive in our hearts. Never forgetting the love she spread.

My younger brother Vince insisted we called him "Vince" not "Vincent" because he too is named after a relative. My uncle Vinny on my father side. I told him he should go by his middle name but he argued. "Patrick is too Irish Brian, I'd rather the Italian side." He had a point. Vince looked the most like my father Eli, they both had this dark wavy hair—just in different lengths. My father ironically had the longer hair, it was nearly to his shoulders. He was just that sort-of guy though. He was very laid back and easy to talk to. He was in his late forties but looked ten years younger & spoke perfect Italian, but you wouldn't know by looking at him. As the years passed Eli taught himself Spanish and Latin as well.

As our family healed from my mother's death, we developed our own pieces of her. Christy might as well have been the princess of Wales. Everyone treated her different, they talked softer to her. She looked just like my mom but with blonde curly hair, my mother's was red. They shared the same bright green eyes, a staple topic strangers loved to acknowledge.

Vince was the "Energy Nazi" as mom was; it isn't exactly what you call fond memories, but we all grieve in our own way. Every time a light was on during day time he would shut it off and open the blinds. Then he'd repeat the same mantra my mother would say.

"What, you don't like the light that God provided for you?"

He is also the world's biggest subliminal smartass, prided on his deep cuts. My brother and I are just over a year apart from each other. Christy was four years younger than I, turning fourteen when Vince was almost seventeen. I was coming to my eighteenth birthday, as well as my senior year of high school and probably the most memorable year of my life.

I was graduating the same day I turned eighteen. May 24th 2008. "Finally I was graduating" I thought. Even though I still had months before then, time passed quickly as we stayed busy. None of us played sports but we had hobbies and chores. By then I had actually done pretty well in school. I was the undefeated champion on the chess club too! Though that isn't saying much, since we only had six members. One of them was a pretentious asshole when I was curious about the club. So I learned chess and signed up for the club just to beat him, over & over again.

My grades were kept high, I was kind of a "goodie, goodie" in school and out of school. I had an "A" in every class but gym. Every other day in gym class my name would be read on roll-call, causing my muscle head of a coach to lose his mind.

"Dickerson"

"Here" a kid replied.

"Laura S."

"Here"

"Vega" The coach said with a pause. "Vega" He said again. "Son of a bitch! Where the hell is Brian Vega?!"

What can say I'm a sucker for love, I ditched for a girl. My girlfriend Angel and I had been together for a year, but she graduated a year before me. She was never the type for college, she was more of a rebel. Angel was the perfect name for her, but ninety percent of that was fallen-Angel. Her parents were junkies so she had her fair share of run-ins with the law. Over the course of her high school years she was arrested for position, larceny and assault three times. All of which she claims were someone else's fault. She was a bit a badass and liked me for some reason. We caught a matinee of a movie after I ditched school.

"Hey Brian." She said whispering as we watched a film.

"Yeah?"

"Why is it in comedies people never just hang out? You know? Something like 'Coming over for diner staring Ryan Gosling' or something stonerish." Angel progressed louder as she talked. "What about when⋯"

"Shut up!" Someone screamed from behind us.

Angel stood up in a rampage. "You got something to say? Huh, shit for brains?" She screamed flipping out her switch blade.

The man backed down & got up with his wife to walk out of the movie. In hindsight I feel bad for the couple trying to enjoy the film, but they should have started with a please be quiet first.

We pretty much just made-out the entire film and got grabby. I wish it were more romantic, but it was worth skipping gym for.

We were opposites but still very alike. Angel was explosive on the outside and sweet around me, I was more reserved, but I had a dark side when need be. Angel said she liked me for my sense of humor. She couldn't stop laughing the day we met. I just commentated on the food aloud in the lunch line my and Angel was behind me. I have a bad habit of saying what I mean uncensored and she found that hilarious. It could have been because Angel was a bit of a sadist, she would laugh if someone hated on anything.

Angel did however fit-in in my family, she came over for dinner often. My dad liked her, but he disapproved of how freely she cursed around Christy.

"Oh girl, I like your hair damn!" Angel said to Christy at the dinner table.

"Thanks, grandpa sent me a curling iron for my birthday." Christy replied softly. "It's everything I ever wanted in a curler."

"Shit, it must be fucking expensive to do that"

"Girls, do you think we can maybe put this on pause for a moment?" Eli said to Angel and his daughter in a firm voice.

"Oh, sorry Mr. Vega!" Angel replied.

Eli sighed and continued saying the blessing for dinner uninterrupted.

Later that evening Angel played video games with Vince, wrestling with him at times to cheat. She loved a good fight, especially when it resulted in someone crying. She had Vince in tears after shutting off his game console, just before losing.

"Oh my God! What are you doing? Are you serious?!" Vince screamed.

"Are you crying right now? It's just a game Vince." Angel said.

"No!" Vince said as he walked towards the door "I'm just really frustrated and you're so mean."

"Vince, wait." Angel ran out after him to make things right.

I don't know what exactly she said that night, but she gave Vince her butterfly knife to atone. He accepted her gift yet held resentment. Angel was not taken well by my family. When she left that night, my father spoke to me in private.

"That girl is nothing but trouble, I can tell you now. She isn't fooling anyone, I won't have to say too much because her type gets bored easy."

"How do you know?"

"Because son, I had a life well before your mother. I'm not proud of it, but that's why I keep you away from uncle Vinny and grandpa Slick."

My curiosity grew to an all-time high. I did not care about his approval for Angel because he was probably right. I just wanted to enjoy the ride a bit longer anyways. Still I wanted to know was more about grandpa Slick. I saw him last at my mother's funeral because my father kept us away from that side of the family. I was never quite sure why. Grandpa Slick looked like he was in the Mexican Mafia and drove the newest trucks. My grandma Betty (Slicks wife) had agoraphobia so she never left the house. She was Italian & loved to cook all day. My dad talked about his mom lovingly, but with sadness. She missed so much of his life by being trapped in the house, prisoner to herself. My father speak about Slick, but only in reference to bad things.

From what I know Slick must cheat on my grandmother, because of when Vince cheated on a test.

I think the quote was "You want to be a cheater like papa Slick?"

My father loved to ask rhetorical questions when we were in trouble. I know Slick has quite a bit of money, but have no idea about what he did for a living. I knew he went to prison as well as my uncle Vinny at one point. There were so many questions but my father over-reacts when I enquire.

"Dad, why won't you tell us about Slick or uncle Vinny? I get if we can't be around them, but why won't you tell us why?"

My father overreacted as I thought he would.

"I have told you why, my family is bad news. Why do you think I can see thorough Angel? Been there, done that. That's all you need to know."

Frustrated I threatened. "Well, if you won't tell me nothing then I will find out for myself when I turn eighteen. Kansas City is only three hours away from here."

It was truly an empty threat because I had no job or car. Dad sold his truck after mom died and took the bus everywhere. We lived in a small town in Kansas called Derby where nothing ever happens.

"Son, you can't go to see them. It's dangerous, seriously. Your grandmother won't even leave the house because of how bad it is where they live."

"Then why does grandpa Slick have new cars if the neighborhood is so bad?"

"Because Brian, Slick makes it bad. Slick has been in charge of some very bad things since I was a boy. Vinny is the same way, he never stopped taking orders from Slick."

I was stunned.

"So wait, my uncle Vinny and papa Slick are gangsters?"

"Yes." Eli replied simply.

"This explains a lot actually, I had this theory before, but I never would have thought it would be real."

"It's real, trust me."

"I'll trust you, if you tell me the truth for a change."

My father took a deep breath and spoke fast.

"Slick lives in a place called Pendleton Heights in KC. He has been in business for decades and runs everything off of Independence Ave. Your uncle Vinny went to prison before you were born for taking the fall for Slick. Vinny has been in and out of lockup several times since then."

Eli continued.

"Listen to son, I left for a reason. Slick is dangerous, he sacrificed his own son for freedom. What does that tell you? Stay away from him Brian."

"Is uncle Vinny like Slick?" I asked reluctantly.

"No son, Vinny is charming to be around. He's funny, witty and kind hearted. He just can't escape the shadow of Slick, he will always be loyal to his father."

I hugged Eli and softly reassured him.

"I love you dad, thank you for telling me the truth, I needed to know."

"I know son."

Vince walked into the kitchen to my father and me in a loving embrace.

"Did I walk in on something?" Vince said pausing at the doorway before looking into the fridge. "Brian, your girlfriend's a bitch."

"Hey, watch that language!" Said Eli.

"Sorry, guess Angel is rubbing off on me. She is a bitch though Brian, we pretend to like her. You're welcome."

Vince grabbed a soda from the fridge and left the kitchen.

"I should have seen that coming." I said.

Eli looked despaired after disclosing sensitive material in our conversation. He went to bed thereafter with his head down. Angel reminded him of some past demons that surfaced.

"Goodnight son."

I couldn't sleep that night. All I could think about was my grandpa Slick. I started day dreaming about him. I couldn't remember what his voice sounded like or if he had an accent when he spoke, but I remembered his face. He had a thick black mustache that extended past his jaw. His hair was medium length and wavy, and of course it was slicked backwards. His stature was solid and his demeanor calm. Somehow I could see the demons in his eyes, I felt a certain pain in his soul like no other.

For some reason, the thought of my grandpa being a killer left me fearless and inquisitive. Did my mother know? She must have, if she married Eli at a young age. My mind wandered loosely, keeping me up all night.

The next morning I awoke to hear Angel downstairs with my family. I was tired and wished to sleep in, but her appearance left me concerned. Especially after the conversation with my father, I was eager to investigate her arrival.

The aroma of delivered pizza filled the air as I opened the door to the outside world. My judgement came into play before going downstairs. I knew Angel was here, so I did not want to talk to her without brushing my teeth. This may be a simple decision for most, but I have a supernatural love for pizza. I could tell just by sent upstairs that this was no ordinary pizza, it was from Luigi's. Facing one of the biggest decisions of my life, I brushed my teeth and greeted everyone.

"Good morning."

"Good morning!" Everyone replied to me.

"Morning? Brian it's the afternoon, we're eating pizza." Vince said.

"Oh, looks like uh, Luigi's huh, looks good."

Angel approached me and gave me a quick kiss.

"Hey babes, are you hungry?"

"No, I'm fine I just brushed my teeth."

"Well, you're missing out, this is some bomb ass pizza. I thought it would make up for last night with Vince."

"Good move! My family loves pizza."

"Son are you not eating?" Eli yelled from across the room.

"No dad, I'm not too hungry and I just brushed my teeth."

"Angel brought your favorite though."

"I know dad, I'm fine though, thanks."

As my luck would have it, Luigi got too old to run the business and closed down within weeks of that Saturday morning. It remains one of the biggest regrets in my life not eating a slice.

Angel helped Christy make cupcakes for desert. I sat and watched superhero movies with Vince and dad, constantly looking back on empty pizza boxes siting at the table. The mail came as my dad started dozing off to the movie, spread out on the couch. Vince went to grab the post from the front door. It was kind of nice that we still had a mailman who delivered to your front door.

Vince shouted from the doorway. "Brian you got mail!"

What could have possibly come for me? It must be a rejection letter from one of the colleges. Vince handed me not one, but three envelopes from the major colleges I had applied to. To my surprise they all said pretty much the same thing.

> Dear Mr. Vega,
>
> We are pleased to inform you that you have been accepted into···

I was accepted into Colorado State, KU and Missouri State. Before then I thought about just going to a Junior College to save money. Ecstatic after reading them, I jumped and woke my dad up from his deep slumber.

"Dad, look, look." I handed my father the sheets of paper. "I got in!"

My father smiled looking over the letters briefly.

"I'm so proud of you Brian, your mother would be so proud."

Through the commotion Christy and Angel came into the living room covered in cake batter, wearing aprons.

"What?" Christy said.

"What is it babe?"

"Brian's moving away to college soon." Vince exclaimed eager to annoy Angel.

"Yay!" Christy screamed clapping. "Way to go Brian!"

Angel wore a happy façade, but it was clear she was not pleased about the news.

"Good for you babe." She said half-heartedly.

We had a mostly awkward night after that. The room felt tense no matter who was in it. It felt like my family was judging me for doing well in school. In actuality, everyone was down at the prospect of losing me, I would miss them as well.

Angel left shortly after frosting the cupcakes and the week seemed to fly by from that moment.

Christy had her birthday, she had a sleep-over with six girls from her school. The main topic of the night seemed to be about boys and how cute they were. I only know because Christy came to me upset that the girls were talking about Vince. He wasn't much older than most of the girls there. He had softer features for a young man and girls went crazy over him.

I consoled Christy assuring her that the young girls had no chance with Vince. This seemed to make her smile. She loved knowing her brother was popular yet loyal. A small part of me wondered why the girls were crushing on Vince and not me. That moment passed quickly, after remembering that I had a girlfriend and they were a bit young for me. I've never seen Vince with a girl before, so maybe he would go after Christy's friends.

Later that week, I found out that Vince had several girlfriends simultaneously. It was a weird phenomenon in high school where I became a dinosaur. My class was on our way out to better things, while Vince's graduating class partied non-stop.

It was under my nose the whole time, he drank and smoked without anyone in the family knowing about it. Vince acted to laid back and smooth. He was never in trouble or got caught. It was too easy for Vince to tell dad he was staying with a friend and then stay out all night. He always came back in one piece unscathed, when asked how it went he would reply "It was okay."

How could I know so little about my own brother? We never really talked much, we lived in an old Victorian style home which was the oldest house on the block. This gave every single one of us our own room, so in a way, we all became loners.

Dad bought the house to be a fixer-upper, but never fixed anything after paying the house off. The attic was unfinished, the second floor had holes in the walls. The roof had damage, so small animals got inside sometimes. Only one of the four bathrooms in the house worked all the way. We could shower on the second floor but there was no toilet, just a board covering where it would go. The main floor was beautiful and finished. My dad's room was on the main floor.

Because the house had so much character, we each decorated our rooms to cover imperfections. In my room I strategically placed my bed over a broken floor-board. There were rock band posters to cover holes in the wall, though it was obvious based on poster location. The posters were scattered on the walls like "Lost pet" print-outs. My room was towards the front of the house so it was the biggest, directly above my fathers.

Christy's room resembled her personality, it was painted pink. She had a reading nook next to a small window overlooking the drive-way. Her bed was petit but plush, there were boy crush posters next to her vanity & unicorns galore.

My father's room had an eerie vibe about it. He kept some of my mother's things, like clothing and makeup. He never re-decorated or changed anything after his wife's death.

Vince's room was most important. His room was on the second floor facing the rear of the house. He had a small window that he snuck out of frequently. It was unnoticed by most how close his window sits to the top of the rear deck. Vince would simply escape by jumping to the roof, climbing down to the deck and walk out through the back yard. It later upset me to find out that Christy knew about Vince before I did. She could easily see him leave from her window. They were closer than I thought as well. Vince stuck up for her on the bus when they were little and it stayed with her. On the outside he looked closed off from the world, but in reality I shut myself off from him.

It felt as though we had a strange family. I had never met Irish-Mexican Italians from the Midwest.

At that time my grandpa Christy happened to be in Dublin, Ireland. He was going to fly in to the states with my grandma Ruth for graduation. It would be guaranteed that he'd be drunk by the time my name was called for diplomas. He kept a flask on him at all times and loved his Celtic gibberish he mixed into drunken conversations. I'm sure he would yell "Slainte" at my graduation. It translates to "Health" but he says it when he takes a drink of whiskey. A Celtic Cheers.

My grandmother Ruth was the sweetest lady in the world. She grew up in North Carolina, but her parents were Irish as well. Ruth could bake bread with the skill of an accomplished baker.

She would insist on cooking every time my grandparents came to visit. She made meat pies and sweet pies the best. I used to love saying that to her. When my mother was alive they visited often, but now every year or so. They blame it on travel, but I think our house reminds them of Alice. Regardless I was excited that they were coming.

Angel became more distant after my acceptance into college. I still had months to choose a school, but she acted as if I already left. I was upset for a moment that passed in a blink of an eye. I was soon out of school, I passed all of my finals and chilled at the house for a week. My siblings still had over a week before summer break. Graduation was only two weeks away and with it, my birthday. The world was beneath me as I floated on a cloud through space thinking about the day. Eighteen was going to be legendary.

My father surprised me early for my birthday one morning before graduation, so I could walk with his present. Eli handed me a small red box. Before I could open it, he wanted to tell a story first.

"Son, you're becoming a man and I want to give you something. Did you know that an acre used to be measured by the distance an ox could pull a plow through a field in a single day? Don't answer, hear me out.   See the ox held the weight of the work on his shoulders, while he kept his head down. He didn't know where he was going, he only knew he was supposed to go there. At the end of the day, an entire acre was plowed by the work of a single animal. I see you in that way. After your mother died you sort of kept your head down. You did what you were supposed to and went far. You didn't see where you were going, but now look at you. You're an ox. Happy birthday son and congratulations."

Inside the box was a golden necklace in the shape of a heart, the back had an inscription.

To our Ox

 Love mom and dad.

My dad explained in a bit further detail.

"It's fourteen carat gold." Eli said. "Your mother got it for you in Dublin visiting grandpa. She told me the story of the ox and how you were an easy child. She talked about how you never cried and how happy you were just being a baby. I got the necklace inscription last week, couldn't wait for you to have it."

I teared up reading the inscription over and over again.

"Thank you dad, I won't let you down."

Just then Vince awkwardly walked by and froze with a blank stare.

"Am I interrupting something? Or, Should I go?"

"Shut up Vince." Eli said, continuing his embrace.

I told my father I choose to go to school in Colorado. I wanted to be an engineer and picked that school, because of the Denver *Broncos*. I loved the mountains as well & the weather.

My dad left for work as the kids left to school. It felt good to be at the house while everyone one else was busy. I took a nap on the couch while watching sitcoms and eating junk food. It was only noon by the time I awoke. There was still three hours before Vince and Christy were home. My dad works a strict nine to five schedule, so he is home at exactly five-forty every day. He would be home sooner, but he chooses to take the bus.

I fell back asleep on the couch and dreamt of my mother. I saw her as if she were still alive. She raised her right hand towards my necklace.

"You will always have my heart."

Slightly freaked out, I opened my eyes and came back to reality. My father said I got jealous when Vince was born, I used to tell my mom to return him to the baby store. Asking her if she loved him more than me, she would reply "You will always have my heart." Somehow that made things better. I was willing to share my mother with my new baby brother from then on. She always knew the right things to say. She watched over me from heaven, I'm sure of it.

Time was frozen, I sat waiting for something to happen. I had few friends, most of which had jobs so life was boring without school or Angel.

As the bus stopped in front of our house to alight children, only Christy came home. I had forgotten about Vince going to his friend's house. He wouldn't be home until dinner. Christy came through the front door and went straight to her room. I tried to speak to her in passing.

"Hey, how was school?"

"Fine." She walked past me, straight to her room.

Teenage girls are so difficult to understand, even if you are a teenager as well.

I started dinner around five o'clock that night, I remember it was Spaghetti Carbonara because Vince came home ecstatic. He ate for two on past nights. He never really gained weight as much as he ate. Even into adulthood, he remained five foot ten and around one hundred-eighty pounds. Time flew by once Vince arrived, from his friend's house. We were joking and laughing non-stop in the kitchen.

When I had finished cooking dinner I called Christy downstairs, Vince and I had already started eating.

"Where's dad?" Christy asked.

"Oh, I hadn't even realized he was late. It's almost six." I said looking at the clock.

"Yeah, I didn't even think anything of it." Vince said.

"Brian, can I use your cell phone to call dad?"

"Sure." I Handed Christy my outdated flip phone.

She retreated to the living room and called Eli worried, as he was never late. She paced back and forth while. Vince and I watched from the kitchen.

"It goes straight to voicemail, I called like nine times." She exclaimed.

"What does that mean?" Said Vince walking to the front door. He looked out the blinds. "This is weird guys, I don't like this."

I could see the concern in my sibling's eyes, Christy was nearly in tears. I had to calm them down.

"Guys, his phone could have died, or he could have missed his bus." I alleged. "Let's give him tell at least seven before we call the fire brigade. If he's not back by eight at the latest we'll worry."

My siblings were retained for the moment, but I was truly panicked within myself. Seven o'clock came with worry, thus eight o'clock provided the panic. By eight-thirty in the evening we received answers in a phone call.

The hospital in the west end of Wichita called looking for me. They informed me that my father had been in an altercation and listed me as his emergency contact. They wouldn't tell me much more than that over the phone, I had to go to the ICU in person. My mind just couldn't seem to grasp the idea that this had happened. It was a shell shock from the way a human should feel. Vince and Christy knew there was something wrong already, but I still had to inform them of the situation. What a torment to lose a parent possibly twice, my mouth couldn't bare such a burden. Vince somehow took my responsibility from me.

"Who was that on the phone? Was it dad? Was it about dad?" Vince asked me glaring deep into my eyes for the slightest glimpse of communication.

I remained silent for a fraction of a second and Vince already figured it out.

"It was about dad, where is he? Is he hurt?" Vince questioned me as fast as he replied to himself. "He is hurt, we need to go."

Vince had perfectly summarized the circumstances we were in, by reading body language and eve movement. This is why I thought he would be perfect for the FBI. Christy burst into tears causing a domino effect. We all became overwhelmed simultaneously sobbing. I held my siblings as they purged all humanity into my arms. I kept repeating that we "had to be strong for dad." Nothing compares to this anguish, feeling helpless and alone. We held each other for strength and came around to our senses. First thing is first, get to Eli. Nothing else matters, he needs us by his side.

The Paths we chose

I called Angel to beg her to let me use her mother's car. Her
phone went straight to voicemail. I forgot she was at work, totally
slipped my mind. Out of options we ran to the bus stop. Vince
and Christy blew past me towards the bus stop, I had fallen
behind.   To my credit, we were running to a connecting bus
ten blocks away. I finally caught up to Vince and Christy waiting
at the bus stop, standing irritated. Public transportation is not for
emergencies, but there were few choices. The bus we took to the
hospital was late ten minutes. So we could have just walked to
the bus stop, instead of running full speed. The irony of urgency
was unbearable for me, I had to just go with the flow. If we took
a taxi it would be around the same time, because we would have
to wait for pickup.

We rode to the hospital silent as statues, the body becomes
useless living inside the mind. I said a prayer and struggled to
not curse at every stop we made along the way. People were
slow to getting on & off of the bus. They held no urgency or care.
We finally arrived to the hospital an hour after our departure.
Time is like a toxicity to the deep thinkers & worriers of this
world. Though I had a chance to calm down drastically.

My hands trembled seeing the state of my father. He was in a comma, hooked up to all sorts of tubes and wires. My siblings and I were allowed to see him at the same time. We shared in a moment of pain viewing the state he was in, how could someone do something like this? Eli was stabbed twice in the back and once in the abdomen. His face was beaten to a pulp with his eye swollen shut. A stench of dried blood emitting from his body fumed through the air. There were a great number of bruises scattered on his body, it looked like a hate crime. We were told that he was unconscious but could still possibly hear us. Vince and Christy said their peace to him as I kept examining the shape he was in.

"Dad? Can you hear me?" Christy asked sobbing uncontrollably. "I love you, please just get better and come home. We need you."

I continued looking for clues to why this happened. His knuckles were bloody and scrapped thin. He must have put up a fight. Since he was stabbed only a few times, I think it happened when he was caught off guard, or there were multiple attackers.

"Dad? Who did this? Why wouldn't you just give up your wallet?" Vince pleaded holding Eli's hand.

Something turned inside me, I knew there was nothing I could do for my father. What I wanted to do was find the people responsible and give proper justice. I was compelled to find answers. There had to be something there, a shred of evidence pointing in the right direction. Years of reading detective comics and super-hero movies about detectives needed to come in handy. Ask the right questions, I kept thinking. Why was his leg broken? Did he fall on it? Or was he hit with a blunt object while down? He had bruises on his arms, I have never seen something like that before. Not even in the movies. There was no way that Eli was punched repeatedly in the arms, who fights like that? That means maybe he was kicked while he was down, or he was trying to protect himself from a blunt weapon.

Vince and Christy laid partially on each side of my father crying through their open prayers. I couldn't seem to weep. I tried, but something about being in that room with my father gave me strength. The "Ox" around my neck meant something. This was my burden to bear, I had to stay strong and keep my head up. The man my father would want me to be.

Like a thief in the night, the devil came to steal my family that night. I heard a voice in the doorway of my father's room.

"Brian, can you step in the hallway for a moment?" asked an officer peaking his head into my father's hospital room.

I abided and left to the hallway, but I could not ignore the substantial instinct in the pit of my stomach. I felt this when we arrived at the hospital, suppose that's reason for the name "Gut

31

feeling". To me it felt like a sensor for evil or danger. I remained quiet to mimic my shell shock from before. I didn't want the cop to know what I was thinking. My eyes met with Vince's line of sight, he could read the worry in my eyes. He understood without words, I needed him to have my back.

"Brian, my name is Officer Jordan. I understand that you are in a sensitive situation right now, but I need you to answer a few questions for me. Can you do that?"

I shook my head up and down signaling my response silently.

"Did your father have anyone who wanted to hurt him? Maybe someone who didn't like him very much."

Again I replied silently shaking my head no.

"Do you have any family members you can stay with? Someone to act as a legal guardian?"

"Yeah, my uncle Vinny or my grandpa."

"Is there any way you can get ahold of one of them? Get them to come down here and talk to me?"

"Yeah of course."

"I'll wait with you until they get here." Officer Jordan said possibly calling my bluff.

My face displayed instant dismay and I lost my poker face. In that moment the officer read me like a book and knew I had no way of reaching out to anyone. Even if I did get ahold of Uncle Vinny or grandpa Slick, there was no guarantee that they would come.

"I'll tell you what, why don't you and your siblings come with me down to the station. We can get ahold of your family and sort this whole thing out."

This concreted my instincts, we were going to foster care. I knew it in my bones. He was going to split us up, I was weeks away from being eighteen too. I would be out of the system quickly, but what about my brother and sister? The cop knocked on the hospital room door to get the attention of my siblings. Looking into my eyes they knew something was wrong.

"Vince, Christy, come here." I said.

The two of them walked to the hallway like they were in trouble. Christy kept her head down wiping tears away, Vince kept looking at me for solutions. The police officer continued with my siblings "Kids, my name is Officer Jordan. The three of you are going to come with me down···"

In that moment I made a life changing decision and knocked the police officer to the ground. I used my entire body weight to slam against him.

"Run!" I screamed at my siblings.

I rushed beside them as they took off in a sprint down the hall towards the elevators. As I caught up to them at the elevators I realized it would be a death trap to wait there. The pissed off policeman was hot on our trial, we had to keep moving.

"Stairs! Take the stairs!" I shouted.

We were only on the third floor of the building. Waiting on the elevator would be pointless. Vince was the quickest among us, nearly leaping down each flight of stairs like a monkey. I stayed around the same pace as Christy. I took pride alone in that, because she had been practicing for track. Going into freshman year she could compete, so she was driven to be fast. We exited the building ninety seconds after my assault on Officer Jordan. On the run my direction faltered as we solely tried to keep up to Vince. After about three blocks of running I screamed ahead at my unexpectedly quick little brother.

"Vince, we need to get off of the street!"

I knew we were pretty far ahead of officer Jordan on foot, but he could catch up pretty darn fast in his police car. Not to mention the other patrol cars he might have alerted. We had a better chance fleeing to somewhere a car couldn't access easily. Vince was once again far ahead of us, thus we followed his lead to a nearby soup kitchen. It had a line wrapped around the block, but

Vince ignored it. He rushed to the front of the line until we caught up to him. I realized the genius in that moment. It looked like we were out of breath homeless kids who missed out on meal time. The three of us waited on the outside of the line for someone to let us cut. Almost immediately someone allowed us to the front of them. We were given a bowl of soup each and a piece of bread.

 The three of us sat towards the back of the old building. It resembled a school cafeteria, but for people in need. At that moment, we were definitely in need and quite hungry.

We heard police sirens pass the soup kitchen several times. Each pass causing more anxiety, I could be jailed and the kids split up. Only one of us was worry free eating his soup. I looked at Vince pounding away at his dinner.

"How could you eat at a time like this?"

"What? "It's good, have you tried it yet?"

He continued thrashing away at his meal with a happy face. My brother was so light hearted, I had to try the soup. After tasting the cabbage soup that the kitchen had provided I was dumbfounded. It was fantastic, simple but layered with flavors. It was exactly what we needed at the time.

Curious I questioned Vince. "How are you so fast?"

"Well; believe it or not Brian, this is not my first time running from the law. Most parties get broken up, and then I run."

It all made sense to me, I was finally getting to know my brother in the strangest of environments. The homeless at the table were very kind to us. They shared stories of places traveled or era's that they lived through. Who knew that someone could boast about just surviving? Surrounded by the answer I was awakened to a harsh reality. The world is a cruel place ready to eat you alive. These people had no one to care for them, out on their own. I felt like we were in this boat with them now. My siblings and I stayed at the shelter for an hour, they even served desert. It was one of the most memorable meals of my life.

The kitchen was open every night from nine to eleven. Supported from local Chefs who donated their time and resources into giving back. It was needed, a hot meal before sleeping cold on the streets. We caught the last bus towards our house. Taking the transportation in the city was never an issue, my father gave us each monthly passes. He hated driving so we'd pair up and take public transportation.

Slightly suspicious that the police would be watching our house, we got out of the bus two stops early. I guess Vince snuck-in quite often, he took a back alley to get through the yard. Then climbed up to his window. We saw multiple police cars staking out the front of the house. I thought that it was a bad idea to return home, but options were nil. I needed to call Angel, but my phone was dead. Plus we had to raid the house for money and supplies. Vince pointed at his window. It was slightly ajar as he always kept it. He leaped over the fence like a natural Tarzan navigating the jungle. Frankly I was amazed at the athleticism of my brother, the kid was borderline parkour.

He opened the tall wooden fence to let us in the yard, leading us through the shadows to the corner of our porch. He then helped Christy and me up to the roof and through his window. It was easier than I had thought and frightening, a burglar could get in quicker. Vince closed his window fully and locked it.

"Keep all the lights off." He whispered. "Get only what you need and let's go to the attic. They could be in here or have a warrant."

"Okay." Christy whispered. "Do you think someone is in the house?"

"No way, but people can see you through windows and hear you."

"Plus, they could get a warrant if they think we're here." I added.

"Well, I'm scared, why can't we just leave? Let's go to Angel's house." Christy said.

"Because, my phone is dead and it's late."

"Can we even trust her?" Vince said. "Angel, I mean. Can we trust she won't give us up?"

"What do you mean? Of course we can trust her."

"Wait I'm kind of confused. Why are we on the run?" Christy asked.

"Because, the state would have split us up. We have no parents."

"I thought we were on the run because you pushed that cop." Said Vince.

"Really?"

"Yeah, totally thought you were crazy. We went with it though."

"Hmm. Do you think they would have split us up?" Christy asked.

"Of course, I'll be eighteen, but not you. Who knows where we would all end up? This was the only choice in my opinion."

"Got to add that in this heart felt moment, we went from whispering to full banter." Vince pressed.

"Right sorry." I whispered again.

The three of us crept our separate ways agreeing only to pack, two days of supplies in a bag. All of us imposing a great amount of stealth putting our belongings in a small bundle. I put a change of clothes, a phone charger, and toiletries in a back-pack.

Christy did almost the same. She had a great deal of candy in her bag, as well as womanly things undiscussed by older brothers. The three of us collected ourselves in the attic of the house. We went over strategy and what we all brought.

I had things like tape, a pocket knife and clothing all in my bag. Christy brought bandages and ointments along with her clothing. Vince brought a double layered pillow case full of non-perishable foods from the pantry. He also ransacked the swear-jar and dads secret stash in his room downstairs. In total, Vince collected over five hundred dollars. When I asked him why he didn't pack clothing. He took off his hoodie showing he was wearing three shirts. He had two pairs of pants on also. The bottom layer was his sweat pants and the top was jeans.

When I finally charged my phone enough to send a message to Angel, I noticed that I already received messages from her.

The messages read:

"The police are here looking for you, where are you?"

"I hope you are safe I heard about your dad."

"The police came back looking for you, they are pretty pissed. Maybe you should keep your distance for a while. It's probably for the best. Love Angel."

I was taken back by what looked like her betrayed. How could she drop me so easily? She put "Love Angel" but not "Love you" there is a difference to me. I actually felt something for her, where as she cast me off like a disease.

"What's next Brian?" Vince asked.

"We need to find uncle Vinny."

"Why?"

"Yeah, Why?" Christy chimed.

"Two reasons, one, he is our closest relative that can take us in. Two, I don't think he knows dad is in the hospital. I'm sure he would want to know about his brother."

"So we are going to Kansas City?"

"I guess so, we need to leave early though. I want to make the first bus out of here. Get some sleep. When the sun rises we leave."

That night I dreamt about my father. I saw him in his work uniform being led by two men. Things went bad and he fought for his life as they both had weapons. The savagery in these men who seemed to know him was unbearable.

That morning I saw the cop car leave, followed shortly by the undercover car leaving. It was nearly five in the morning, either shift change or coffee break disrupted the stake-out. We seized the opportunity and left through the front door. Then a bus ride all the way to the bus station. I bought us each a one way ticket to Kansas City, Missouri. Using cash that Vince provided from our house raid.

It felt like an adventure setting off to an unknown city, in search of family treasure. We were stocked with rations and our own unique emergency kits. The bus departed around nine a.m. My siblings were still tired from the commotion of the past twenty-four hours. They fell asleep instantly after leaning their heads together. The ride was an eight hour trip, almost triple the time of a car ride.

I took that time to think about my family that we were searching for. My uncle Vinny looked like a cross between me and my father, I could spot him easily. Though it had been so long since we had last seen each other, I wondered if he'd even recognized me. As for my grandpa Slick, he was a gangster, but we were still family. Surely he missed us, he had to have missed dad. What would he do finding out about Eli being in a comma? How would I even find him? I planned to follow what my father had disclosed to me. They both lived off of Independence. Maybe if we asked around in that area, someone would know him. I slept easy those eight hours, through the pit stops and smoke breaks. I was excited to find our long lost family so it did not bother me sitting next to a stranger. Vince and Christy shared adjoining seats, so they were well entertained.

Arriving in Kansas City was overwhelming at first, we had no idea where to head. We found our way to Independence Avenue towards the Pendleton Heights province. The area had an old Chicago vibe about it. The houses were all large and laid with brick. Most places had bars on most windows. The city seemed empty in these parts, those who were outside had a rough demeanor to them. Made of grit from years of hardship.

 The buildings were mostly old Victorian homes or projects, there was no middle ground. It would be a shot in the dark, but we made it. Grandpa couldn't be far, and this was his exact neighborhood.

First we started looking for a place to stay for a couple nights. There were only two motels close to the area that we found. The first motel denied us because I was under age with no credit card.

The second place brought us some luck, so I paid in advance for three nights in cash. The man who worked there didn't seem to care about anything but money. It was clear that this was the place men took hookers. We saw a few coming into the building in fact, thought it didn't matter. The place had a certain odor to it that lingered in each room. Sort of a cigarette stench mixed but sweaty socks.

Our room had only one bed and the floor was sketchy. Dark red carpet, but parts were spotted salmon colors. We'd rather share the bed, then take biohazard risks.

The walls were forest green with pictures of the beach hung around. As if green reminds someone of the beach, a toddler could decorate better. We deiced to sleep foot to head back-to-back on the bed. It was the only way we could make it work. The city looked dangerous so I thought we shouldn't go out past dark. It was getting late just finding the hotel. We still had snacks, but not much after the bus ride. Vince is a bottomless pit that devours everything in sight. No wonder we were low on snack. He ate ravioli straight from the can on the bus, what a madman. Christy had mostly candy left in her bag, I was hungry, but not for sweets. I needed a deli sandwich in my life to drown away my sorrows, eating my feelings. I decided to walk a couple blocks to the corner store for drinks and supplies.

"I'm going to run up the street to get some food. Can you just chill out and watch Christy for a minute."

"Why don't we all go? It would be safer."

"Because I will be quick and someone needs to stay here."

"Brian can you get me some chocolate?" Christy asked.

"More? Really? Sure, I'll be right back."

"What about soda? Can you grab some soda?" Vince said.

"Fine, lock the door, don't let anyone in."

Vince continued.

"Then how will I know if you're knocking or someone else?"

"I'll do a secret knock that only you and I will know.   Like this, three hard knocks and two soft ones."

"What if someone actually knocks like that? Then what? Then I look like an idiot for letting in a serial killing stranger."

"Shut up! Look there's a damn peep hole on the door. Just see if it's me when you hear a knock. You think you can do that?"

"Well of course B-rye I'm not stupid." Vince said pressing my patience, reminding me he was my younger brother.

"Seriously?" I raised my eyebrows like they were pistols. "Wow, just watch Christy I'll be back."

Leaving the motel revealed more signs that we were in a shady area. There was an adult store next door with a full parking lot. I walked with haste past drunken homeless and stray dogs barking. No eye-contact was made, simply a guy walking to the store. The streets were littered heavily with graffiti staining the walls of buildings. To me the markings looked like meaningless symbols, produced by illiterate morons looking for attention. Getting to the run-down corner store took all of five minutes to walk to, but that was a long five minutes. Paranoia of being mugged was relevant to my location. This was going to be a, get-in, get-out kind of thing.

The inside of the store was cluttered, it took longer navigating through half empty boxes, than it did to walk to the store. I bought us enough food to last three days. It filled two paper bags full of junk food. I still had forty dollars left and three days to find my uncle. Things were starting to look up, maybe dad would wake up by then. I looked at the middle-eastern man behind the cash register. He looked tired and unhappy, this was not the American dream he envisioned. Behind the counter of a corner store, in the heart of the ghetto.

"Excuse me, sir?" I bothered him for a moment. "Have you heard of Vinny Vega? Or Big Slick?

"Is this some rap group? We don't sell cd's here."

"I'm sorry, forget I asked."

I shrugged it off and paid for the groceries. This might be harder than I thought, how was I going to find my uncle if nobody knew him? I left the corner quickie mart with a clouded mind. All I could think of was the massive undertaking before me. I ignored my surroundings walking past the dangers of man with ease.

About half a block from the motel I heard a voice shout at me. Out of the corner of my eye I saw three men rushing my side. Instinctively I turned to face them still holding two grocery bags.

The thought of running slid through my mind. I was so close to the motel, I could make it easy. The problem is if they had guns, I would be leading them to my siblings. Putting Vince and Christy in direct danger. I held my ground instead, with a fearless façade to imitate a braver man.

"What up homie where you from?" Said a thug.

"I'm just passing through I don't want any problems."

There were three thugs, but only one of them spoke to me.

"You don't get to decide what you want. You're on our turf now. What you got in the bag?"

"Food, My food." I said deepening my voice. I searched for a way out of the situation while they drew near to me.

"You're food? Nah homie you got it wrong, you're holding my food. NOW HAND IT OVER!"

The thugs looked like teens themselves, maybe I had a chance fighting. The one that spoke to me was Latin-American of some sort and the other two were African-American. They dressed similar, though doubtfully intentional. All of them had white shirts of some form, short hair and khaki shorts. It felt like a shakedown from the associates of the "Gangster Gap Store"

"Screw you, I don't have time for this." I said calmly.

I just started walking away like nothing had happened, that was my mistake. Turning my back I was attacked all at once, barraged with fists flying in every direction. The grocery bags finally fell to the ground, scattering the contents. I raised my arms to protect my head from injury. My ears began ringing from a direct blow to my temple. My vision started to slip, I needed to act fast before they beat me to death. In utter confusion I swung my arms wide, hoping to connect flesh to knuckle. Through pure chaos I landed two powerful strikes to one of the thugs. He fell to the earth giving me a surge of adrenaline and hope for escape. Now only contending with two sets of hands, I stood up straight. We went toe to toe. I landed enough hits to discourage them, they clearly did not expect such a fight.

Subsequently it was not worth it to them anymore, the muggers grabbed most of the spilled groceries and ran away. They left behind some instant noodles and some candy bars. I scooped up the remains and shuffled to the motel in agony. My head was throbbing uncontrollably and I couldn't tell where blood was coming from.

Knock, knock, thump, thump.

I tried to mimic the secret signal we had, but received no answer.

Knock, knock, thump.

Again no answer.

Knock, slam, thud.

Vince finally approached the door and spoke from the other side.

"That's not the password, can't let you in, no way, no how" Vince said in a surly voice.

"Vince can you stop quoting the old movies, it's not funny, just open the door please."

Secretly I thought his impression was hilarious and I held in laughter. He unlocked the door and opened it smiling, then his face turned to shock.

"Holy shit Brian, what happened to you?"

"Nothing, I'm fine."

Christy ran to me hugging me, her eyes were filled with tears.

"What happened Brian? I want to go home."

"Everything is fine, you should see the other guys."

Vince paced back and forth in fury.

"This is bad man, this is real bad." He said in a high pitch voice. "How does this keep happening? What the hell is wrong with people? I'm sick of this, first dad then you."

"Calm down, we knew this area was dangerous. I even said we shouldn't go out past dark. It's my fault this happened. I should have just followed my own advice. That being said let's just make the best of it, I'm still standing Vince." I smiled wide.

"Christy, your brother is seriously losing it. Brian, you're clearly going insane."

"Well maybe so," I pulled out the candy that made it back. "I got your chocolate Christy, that's what really matters." I smiled again to make light the shape I was in.

Christy miraculously stopped crying and snatched the chocolate bars from my hand. It was amazing what a little sugar could do.

"Now, if you'll excuse me I've had a long day & would like a shower." I expressed walking into the bathroom.

"Hey, where's the soda?!" Vince shouted into the door, realizing he had been left out.

"Shit out of luck!" I shouted back through the door.

The motel restroom was the bare minimum for hygiene. Shower, toilet sink and one bar of soap. That's all you found in the bathroom. The mirror was covered in a thick film that made it mostly blurry. I had a cut on my forehead that blead down to my eyes. It had a pathway like a river, undisturbed and narrow. The side of my lip was fat and tender. I tapped my face in different areas because it felt numb. I smiled into the mirror and saw my mouth was covered in blood. I rinsed out my mouth multiple times and washed my face with the bar of soap. Looking at my clean face I looked unscathed from battle. The moment felt like a small victory for surviving what life threw at me. Vince's insanity argument looked like a real possibility because I felt invincible. My right ear began ringing again so I turned my head for inspection. It was bleeding and bright red. This enraged me on the inside, I had to find these sons of bitches and catch them off guard. A hot shower was needed, but not what the motel offered. Saying "the shower ran cold" would be an understatement. The shower had only the temperature of ice. It was meant for quick sanitation, or the gas bill was late. It was the quickest I think I ever bathed in my life.

Standing in the bathroom I glared into the mirror at my own reflection. Be the Ox, I thought. Vince and Christy could know the truth about what happened, but not what I had planned next. Pride was on the line this time, what if they see me again? What if those thugs come at me when I'm with Vince or Christy? No chance I was going to let that happen, they had to be taught a lesson. Never mess with a Vega, never rattle the Ox.

I pictured the image of an Ox in my head. He had great power, but kept his head down working. He was doing what he was supposed to do, then I pictured an evil farmer. The farmer whipped and provoked the Ox, he was cruel to the beast. This set off an untapped rage inside the animal directed at the farmer. The Ox had a new burden, killing the farmer and destroying everything he had built. I follow the rules and keep my head down. But they were cruel to me, they had to see the beast.

My emotions stayed hidden while I returned to Vince and Christy after my shower. I explained fully what happened. They were distraught, but we unwound and eventually fell asleep. I however faked sleep, to be left to my mischievous ways. I put on a dark oversized hoodie grabbed my small pocket knife. There was a minimal chance that the thugs would still be out, or even in the neighborhood. I still bet on the fact that maybe they lived close, maybe they saw an outsider as an easy target. The night grew parasites. There were more people out at two o'clock in the morning, then there were midday. I had my pocket knife already open leaving the motel, but something better presented itself. There was a metal blunt object on the ground, how tempting? Almost like a gift, I picked it up. It was hollow and super lightweight, perfect for a hard swing. Further inspection showed it was a chair leg to a motel room, I slid the bar up my sleeve &moved up the street like an addict, stiff and sporadic. This was my camouflage from the enemy, I needed to blend-in. To my surprise, the gang was still on the corner, only in greater numbers. Just two of the muggers were there, the main one who spoke was absent. Either way I was sure to make a lasting impression on the unsuspecting crew. Slowly I crept closer to the group with my head down until I was in standing in front of them.

"What's up homie, you looking to buy?"

Without hesitation I released the bar from my sleeve to my grip and swung like Babe Ruth on game day. The metal leg was quite useful, in one swipe I struck two men. Within seconds I had taken the entire group to the ground with fractured bones. Those who tried to get back up were quick to receive strikes from the steel and myself. There was no way in hell I would lose to these punks twice. The group started to flee, separating like oil in water. The last two I remembered from earlier, they staggered to grab a hidden bag from underneath a dumpster. Suddenly a gun flew in my direction out of the bag. It was a mistake made from snatching the unzipped bag swiftly & carelessly.

I lunged at the gun but there was no rush. They left behind the gun and their bag. Guess it's "mine now" I tossed the gun in the bag and looked to see who was watching me. As I scanned the area fully it dawned on me, not a single soul cared. Everyone was more focused on not being seen themselves, they too were up to no good. Now in an unforeseen high, I strolled to the motel with glee. There was a mystery bag in my possession and a gun. Oh how excited I truly was, like a child on Christmas day. There could be anything in that bag, money, drugs or even more guns.

Sneaking back into the room was surprisingly easy, Vince and Christy remained peacefully asleep. I retreated to the picturesque bathroom of the slummed motel to raid the goodie-bag. Unfortunately there were only tiny baggies of drugs in the mystery bag. At the time I thought they were filled with cocaine. There was no way I was going to sell drugs, but I couldn't throw it away either. So I looked for hiding places. The ceiling to the motel luckily had drop tiles that could move. I stood on the toilet and shimmied the tile to the side. Then I shoved the bag into the ceiling. It would live there until the day it was useful. The gun was to stay with me, I needed it for protection. One day in this city and it already felt like I ran it. I studied the gun in great depth, though it was a simple revolver. Six bullets, six shots I thought. Okay, safety-on, safety-off. There was no serial number on the gun, it was removed.

I had never fired a pistol before, but the way things were going I'm sure I'd get some practice. My father was an expert marksmen with a rifle, but he never showed us how to shoot.

Aloud I spoke "point and shoot" aiming the revolver into the mirror at my reflection. This gun was probably used in several murders. What kind of gun is untraceable? A murder weapon with no prints or digits, right? This was all speculation I gathered from watching gangster movies with my father. One of the best scenes I can remember from a gangster movie is about the untraceable gun. With tape on the handle and hammer, the gangster explains how it's perfect for a hit. Slick was a gangster, my Uncle Vinny is also. It was curious to ponder if it ran in the family, was I born a criminal?

As glamourous as it may sound, I wanted the opposite. I wanted to go to college and be someone great to help others. Truly it was all to help my family, I desired the best for them. Maybe if I were a doctor or engineer then Vince would follow in my footsteps. Christy would be steady behind Vince, staying far ahead of the curve. Instead I held a pistol in my hand thinking of my father. This was the path that I chose, one of great sorrow for not putting my head down. The family might have been fine living apart in foster care. My father could have healed and taken back custody. There were too many variables to consider. At the time I was not thinking straight, Officer Jordan was a good man. He was just doing his job and I over reacted.

Now were on the run fighting to survive, and it's all my fault. My mind wandered in dark directions so I hid the gun under the sink. No one would look there because, why would they?

Tomorrow was a new day, it couldn't possibly get worse. My siblings fell to sleep with ease. They sprawled out on the bed, leaving not an inch for me to rest. Without fear or sanity I slept on the floor that night.

It felt relaxing lay out, my body was sore everywhere. I just wanted to repose and stretch my legs before a day full of searching.

Hardship & Friendship

I woke up to Vince and Christy fighting at an unattainable pitch for normal humans. My head was pounding something fierce. Blood had dried inside my ear falling out like loose ear wax. My face felt like putty when I touched it, like I could reshape it into someone else's facade.

"What are you fighting about?!"

Reluctantly I opened my eyes, Vince had a candy bar in his hand. He was trying to shut Christy out of the bathroom so he could eat it.

"Brian, it's the last of my chocolate! He's going to eat it." Christy said, as she was shut out of the bathroom.

I was irritated and sprung up to yell at Vince, I vaulted to the bathroom door roaring to my brother.

"Vince, give her back the candy. You know how much it means to her."

"Screw that!" Vince said through the door.

56

"Excuse me?! I will break down this door, if you don't give Christy back her candy."

"Brian we didn't eat anything last night." Vince said through the door. "You lost the money and the food, but brought back freaking candy for Christy. She ate like six pieces of candy, you need to let me have this one!"

Christy looked at me awaiting my response.

"Well, I can't argue with that."

Casually I walked to the empty bed and went back to sleep, I was merely a mediator and judge. Vince was right, hell I was hungry at the time as well.

"Brian you're going back to sleep? Wake up! Wake up now!"

"No⋯" I muttered. "Shut-up." I said to my sister.

The argument was over as far as I was concerned, sleep was priority. Six hours later I was woken up by fighting yet again, this time I was at fault.

"What are we still doing here? I am so ready to go home." Vince Exclaimed.

"Brian can we just go home?" Christy said to me as I awoke.

"How? We have no money."

"What happened to looking for Uncle Vinny and grandpa? You slept the entire day! It's almost seven." Vince exclaimed.

"I couldn't sleep last night. So I walked around for a while."

"Brian, why the hell would you leave again?" Christy said.

"You see that, you're making Christy, sweet Christy curse."

"Oh, sweet Christy does more than that." She replied.

I was disgusted and plugged my ears, while my sister pulled my arms away.

"Not like that Brian, unplug your ears."

"Okay"

"Why would you leave the room after getting mugged?" Vince asked.

"We don't have food Vince. What if we get stuck here longer than a couple days? Motel rooms don't pay for itself either."

"Oh, so you got our money back?" Vince said.

"No, not quite."

"But, you got food?"

"No, I didn't get food either."

"So what did you get?"

"Vince leave him alone."

"No, I'm not going to leave him alone because we are here over him. I'm all for wild goose chases, but you have to start them Brian! Christy and I have been sitting here starving all day while you slept. It sucks that they beat you up, but you went out alone. Not once, but twice last night. We followed you here because we love you, not so we could watch each other. Brian you need to get your shit together, foster care looks good right now. They might try to fondle me there, but damn I'll be fed at least." Vince ranted in fury.

"Look, I'm sorry Vince. They kicked my ass, I'll admit it. I should have just stayed here, but I left. When you guys fell asleep it was eating at me. I had to do something."

"Had to do something? You could have been killed Brian, doesn't that register to you?"

"Yeah, but I won the second time."

"You won?" Christy asked.

"What the hell does that mean? You're missing the point, I feel like your freaking mom right now." Said Vince

We sat in silence for a moment, it was clear that hungry was clouding our moods.

"Okay, so the second time I left I had my pocket knife. It was stupid, but it's all I had. When I left there was a metal rod from a chair outside, it was better as a weapon. I slid it up my sleeve and beat the shit out of that gang with it."

Astonished Vince questioned me further.

"How many was there? How did you get so close? They weren't carrying anything?"

I explained the rest to my siblings, there was no point hiding it. I even showed them the gun and where the drugs were. We had to be transparent with one another.

I couldn't rightfully protect my family, if I was the one who put them in danger. We had to do this as a group, they had my back when I pushed the cop and ran. We were stronger in numbers as well as smarter. Vince had a natural street savvy like none other. He could sense danger a mile away. For our survival we had to work together as a unit. We had no money, no car, and no home. The only way out of this shit was through the mud.

The gun symbolically brought us closer together. We had this false safety net with it. My brother and sister knew it was bad, but they were not against us having it. They were supportive of the fire-arm. With that gun we could get out of almost any situation, but have to live with the consequences. Indeed it would be a blood oath to sell your soul for freedom. The revolver was a quill to the ink, waiting for blood.

The day had all but passed and we were outstandingly hungry. Vince formulated a plan for us to score some food. It was dark, he advised that Christy pretend to be pregnant using ratty shirts. The shirts would pay for the food, in a sense because she would ditch the extra shirts for food. Christy added to the plan that she could keep the shirts and just take enough for the night. She also wanted distractions so she wasn't caught red handed. It was crazy even thinking about stealing, devising a heist level operation for chips. We had every second memorized because we had never stolen anything.

The heist went as follows:

Christy enters the corner mart. Fifteen seconds later Vince and I show up. The guy at the register remembers me from last night. I spark up a conversation while Vince looks suspicious intentionally. All eyes are on us as Christy cleans house with anything she can grab. The back of the store had sandwiches, those were the main objective. Christy leaves after one minute, and we follow thirty seconds later. Then back to the motel to enjoy the spoils.

It was a flawless plan to us, we wrote it and practiced in the room. Hunger does some strange things to the body. We thought we were unstoppable, if the gang started trouble then flash the gun. If we get caught stealing, run or show the gun. We had a get out of jail free card we thought ironically. Jail is where it could also put us.

The time came to execute the plan, we were well prepared, ready for action. Close to ten o'clock with a full moon illuminating the sky. We dashed down the block as if we owned every building. This place didn't seem so scary and people seemed to keep to themselves. Even Christy wearing Vince's oversized sweater fit in. As we came up to the corner store I saw a familiar face coming out of the store. It was the Latino guy who robbed me last night, he wasn't with the others when I went back. All at once he noticed me with Vince and Christy. He smiled as if he knew something I didn't, my siblings were unaware that this was the guy. Slowly, yet casually, I lifted my shirt just slightly enough to show the pistol tucked away. He ran in the opposite direction, this alerted Vince to his identity.

"Was that one of the guys?"

"Yeah." I said laughing.

"Did you show that sum'bitch the heat?" Christy said.

"Really? Go back to being a little girl!"

"Sorry, the only channel we have plays wrestling."

Vince laughed, proud of his younger sister. She was learning his ways.

"Okay, is everyone ready to go?" I asked.

"Affirmative captain." Vince said.

Christy entered without us, so we were off count.

"1, 2, 3, 4⋯" We spoke together.

"Wait, maybe we shouldn't count aloud." I said.

"Yeah, you're right. We can't slip up on stupid shit, no getting side tracked. I hope she gets cheese puffs though⋯"

"The sandwiches are the main objective, we cannot waste baby room on cheese puffs!"

"Just saying, they sound good right now."

"Yeah, they sure do, I could eat anything."

"Oh! A cheeseburger sounds awesome right about now, all melty with a large order of fries."

"Vince, it's been well over fifteen seconds we have to go. Now all I can think of is food, thanks."

"You're welcome."

"What? Ugh, c'mon let's move."

We rushed inside behind of schedule. Christy was out of sight, Vince and I spread out to attract attention. It was too obvious how loud my brother was, he wasn't meant for acting. The cashier was different today then yesterday. To him I must have looked crazy with a busted up face strolling around. Christy needed a distraction so I went to strike up a conversation, but another customer was ahead in line.

"Hey Omar." The man said.

"Tanner, my homie. What's happening man?"

The two carried on the conversation and I was left awkwardly in the isle. This Tanner guy looked like he was from the area, but also resembled someone in Derby. Tanner was wearing a white tank-top with a, oversized "G" silver necklace. He had one visible tattoo of broken heart on his neck. I veered from the original plan worried, I signaled Vince to abort the mission. We went to the back of the store to look for Christy, but we couldn't find her. Panicked we left in different directions, Vince stumbled on a promotion stand, knocking over tons of chips. It was clear that we were together and up to no good. Any idiot could spot that from a mile away.

Omar stared at the door in amazement while we left. He hadn't a clue what we took, in fact Vince and I took nothing. Tanner gave the man forty dollars cash so he would not call the police. He told him we probably needed what we took.

As we rushed outside Christy was waiting for us with an entire womb full of treats for us.

"What took you guys so long?"

"How'd⋯"

"How did I what? It was easier than we thought. I left right after you guys walked in, it took like thirty seconds."

"All hail the king." Said Vince.

I was strangely proud of her for being such a natural. We walked back to the motel with much haste for the multiple crimes we may have committed. If this were an actual heist, we would have been filthy rich. Christy had drinks, sandwiches, chips and candy. The holy grail of quickie shop munchies, this was one for the books.

It was like we discovered hidden talents about each other. Vince was an escape artist who could get out of any situation, or into any building. Christy was quick and savage with thievery, there isn't another way of putting that. As for me, I fought back. Each and every time someone pushes I fight back. Come at my family, expect a fight. Hurt me while I am outnumbered and you better watch your back. We slept easy that night, all fitting snug into a single bed. Our stomachs were full, it was junk but we ate. Full on success we had a plan for the next day, wake up early and find grandpa. Easy as pie.

Christy prayed aloud. "Dear God, please help us find grandpa and Uncle Vinny. Heal my father please, and let us come home. We just want to go home. Amen."

The following day we finished the snacks Christy stole for breakfast. We searched together up and down each block for grandpa's house. We've been there before but it was years ago, too long for me to remember exactly. We asked strangers if they knew who he was, Slick or Uncle Vinny. No one knew the Vega name at all or had a clue who we were asking about. The day was a loss, a complete failure. Our resources were completely exhausted, who was left to ask? By this time tomorrow the entire neighborhood would know us. Though our resilience was senseless, we were working towards an impossible task to begin with. Even my phone had given up on and broke before noon. We had to find him, I thought. We had to.

Once again my siblings were hungry without hope on our last night at the motel. There was no money to pay for an extra night's stay either. We went to the corner store for more food, but with an alternate approach. We sent Christy in to get the food while we waited, this time we would act as protection for her.

Christy entered the store with her frizzy hair peeking out of the hoodie. I could see her from door outside slightly. The better view was that of the cashier, I could fully see him and his line of sight. Again I saw that Tanner guy talking to him when Christy passed. He was very aware of Christy and what she took. As my sister left the store I saw Tanner point to her leaving. He pulled out some cash and handed it to the cashier.   Why did he do that? I was so taken back, it distracted from Vince and Christy running. They reached the motel door before I was half-way there. My little sister had snatched more than before, it might have actually been worth more than what Tanner paid. We enjoyed our junk food and cold sandwich supper thanks to our fantastic sister. I remained baffled by the Tanner guy, maybe I was mistaken in what I saw. Why would he help a stranger?

 I wondered, peacefully drifting to sleep that night carelessly optimistic.

Again the next morning, Christy, Vince and I went searching for our family. We never took the same street twice, we could cover more ground this way. The houses all looked the same, but I could picture my grandfather's house in my head. We just needed to find it.

The three of us brought our belongings with us, it would be useless to return to the motel. We were broke, the pressure was on to find Slick. It became routine to ask every soul possible if they knew him. A picture would be better, but we did not have one. We were positive throughout the day, joking about our harsh reality. I would say something like "We can stay here for the night." Sitting next to a dumpster. As we walked past an old train yard I would say "What about here?" jokingly. Vince and Christy thought the bit was hilarious. The fear of having nowhere to sleep at night somehow turned to humor. I had to make light of the situation, but it dawned on me to scout possible forts for real.

We brainstormed on how to make money during the search. My idea was to get quick jobs like helping at a gas station for an hour. We were officially homeless and crazy wondering the streets. Christy had the idea that we could beg for change and by the end of the day, have enough for a meal. I brought up the fact that we had no money for a sign. Why do the homeless have an unknown permanent-marker budget? Vince suggested that he teamed up with his sister to beg, he thought they had more pull together. Additionally, Vince wanted me to stay out of it. He thought my presence would ruin the helpless child vibe.

Sadly that was as far as our ideas went. I was still an infant when it came to hustling, I couldn't make something from nothing. The thought did cross my mind that we could try to sell the gun. My siblings and I all agreed, it would be too much of a hassle to attempt selling illegal firearms to survive. We agreed only to use it for our own protection. The revolver was worth more to us then food, it meant safety. Vince and Christy were probably worried, but they knew I'd use the gun.

If it came down to a matter of life or death, I choose life. I wanted to live and didn't think that was selfish. Above that, I wanted to protect my family. The thought of losing another family member was terrifying to me. There was no other choice but to keep the weapon. It was night in the blink of an eye, we had failed once again. Now it was time to focus on survival, we had to find a place for the night. We back-tracked to the old abandoned train yard that I pointed out earlier mockingly. It was perfect for the homeless, there were three empty carriages open. The rest of the train vessels were locked. The train yard had an eerie fog and rotting aroma radiating from the soot. I would believe it if the train yard was haunted, the hair stood up on the back of my neck just thinking about it. We had to jump a chain-link fence to get to railway, but it was easy. None of us had trouble hopping over the fence, we ignored the boundaries like they were suggestions. Vince ran ahead of Christy and me to inspect the carts. The three open carts were empty, two of them smelled horrible though. The third cart had hay left behind. It must have hauled livestock previously, but it felt perfect for us.

Vince jumped into the train cart and kicked the hay into a pile to sleep on. We were all exhausted after spending yet another day searching in squalor. I helped Christy assemble a bed of hay for her, I made one for myself as well. We attempted to close the sliding door on the cart, but it was welded open. How was this yard not crawling with the homeless? Did they really respect the fence? It was a mansion compared to sleeping on the sidewalk and we were prepared to sleep in shifts if that happened. Instead the train yard provided comfort and warmth when we needed it most. It was like God was on our side looking out for us. Maybe my mom was my guardian angel helping me rise to the occasion.

No tears were shed that night, we were still nostalgic at our luck. We reasoned with each other. How could we make it here and not find grandpa? How did I get a motel underage? Why was the train yard so perfect to sleep in? We had to be here for a reason. Nothing happens without a reason, we thought. Life was too tragic to remain in discourse, we could rise from failure, having true faith. Vince and Christy were going to pan handle in the morning. As for me, I was to look for quick work. Anything to make a buck.

I showed Christy and Vince the gun and how to use it, as though I were an expert. I figured they could keep it staying in one location, use it if necessary. I was looking for honest work, the gun would do me no help. Besides it felt good knowing my little sister was safe. There was a grocery store within walking distance from the train tracks. Vince and Christy would just ask for change with a paper cup we took from the motel. If they felt in danger, they were to run back to the train. The plan sounded simple, but had plenty of room for error. We had no other option but to survive fending for each other. There wasn't a way to tell time, instead we planned to watch the sun. When it was highest in the sky we would all know to return to the train. They both understood the severity of messing up. It was time to get serious, we had to grow up.

When daylight broke I was the first awake, so I woke the others and departed. I hopped back over the fence and headed towards the original corner store we stole from. It seemed like karma needed to be fixed there for theft. When I left it was cold, my hands were shivering frantically. I moved at a fast pace to warm up my body. Hopefully Vince and Christy would be doing their thing soon. Any little bit would help at this point, we were refraining from stealing our meals. We shrilled towards the thought of living like *Aladdin*, we're not riff-raff or street rats.

My determination for working at the corner store was flawless. I envisioned my pitch walking the store. Just five dollars to clean the entire store, ten to stock it. I thought it was worth a shot to try. Worst that could happen is the guy says no, then I find another business.

I saw something strange just before arriving by foot to the old corner store. There were two groups of guys in a vacant parking lot. The first group was leaned up against parked cars, there were only three of them. It caught my eye that Tanner was amongst the smaller group. Clearly they were in a meeting with the others in broad daylight. His friends looked like twins almost, they shared the same clueless expression. All three of the men were Caucasian in a dominantly African American neighborhood. What the hell was going on? It was too early for drug dealing, curiosity got the better of me.

The second group were covered in tattoos, there were five of them. Four of them stood behind their leader, from a distance I could see he had a black eight-ball tattooed on his neck. The man was light skinned with a shaved head and heavy build. He had a good amount of muscle on him, standing between six' two, six' three. When he turned his head I saw his emotion turn wild.

Tanner was only around five' eleven at most. He had a very slender build about him, but he looked comfortable. The Eight-ball guy starts yelling at Tanner. His crew abandons him running away in fear, while he held his ground. I expected him to flee like the others, he was all alone but he stayed. Tanner ripped his shirt off and started swinging on all of them. He didn't give them a chance to throw the first punch. He hit like a boxer, very precise. He moved like he was trained to fight from birth, though he still took some damage. This was full-on war by this point.

I had so much respect for this guy, I had to help him. With a burst of adrenaline I rushed to his aid. I was going to win by any means necessary, I was not afraid to fight dirty outnumbered. Especially with my recent experience in fighting. I went straight for the guy with the eight ball on his neck. It caught him off guard being punched from behind. He was taken back by a stranger stepping in. The bout was sloppy for me, I felt like I was caught up with the big guy the whole time. Eight-ball wasn't taken down without effort.

We swapped equal amount of blows, my surprise attack was in vain. The guy recovered too easily, I was hitting him in the face with all my might. It only irritated him, causing him to unleash a flurry of combinations. He knocked the wind out of me first, with a wicked left hook. This was followed by his knuckles cracking my jaw. I fell to the pavement hazy and weak. I spat out the taste of blood, one of my back teeth was knocked completely out. He messed me up good, but I wasn't dead yet. I reached out and grabbed his leg from the ground, it caught his attention. He shifted his body back towards me and I struck him in the groin. Again and again I hit him in balls until he fell on the ground with me.

"Now you're on my level bitch!"

I crawled on top of him and tore his face apart, until he was unconscious. Tanner grabbed me from behind and pulled me off of my opponent. The gang had ditched eight-ball, it was poetic justice. I guess there is no honor among thieves, or maybe they weren't thieves. Tanner looked like he could have handled the fight by himself. He was wicked fast and handled four guys alone. Tanner did not have a single mark on his face or body from the fight. Meanwhile my face was being molded into sloth from *The Goonies*. How was this guy so fast and skilled? He must have fought professionally.

Tanner sat on the ground next to me and lit a cigarette. He was exhausted too, he offered me a cigarette without saying anything. He opened his pack and leaned it towards me with his arm stretched wide. I needed to smoke after a fight like that, there were no other trophies. He lit my cigarette, which happened to be my first one. I puffed away without inhaling, smoking was easy I thought. Tanner leaned back with his natural swagger and attempted to read my intensions.

"I've seen you around."

"Oh yeah?"

Soon after I actually inhaled the cigarette on accident. I started coughing uncontrollably, smoke felt terrible in my lungs. Who would do this to themselves?

"Are you okay dude?" Tanner said patting my back. "You don't smoke huh?"

"No, not really."

"That makes sense, you look kind of young. How old are you?"

"Eighteen, well almost eighteen."

"Almost, ha-ha I like that dude. Well guess I'm twenty-six and a half."

His playful smile let me know it was okay to laugh, he wasn't being harmful.

"Whew, that was fun huh kid?" He continued.

"I wouldn't say fun, you do this for fun?"

"Sometimes." Tanner said laughing.

He took another rip of his cigarette and stood up. He extended his hand to assist me up from the asphalt. "What's your name bro?"

"Brian Vega. . . What about you?"

"Tanner Brady."

"Pleasure to meet you."

"We should probably get out of here before more of his goons show up."

He was probably right, the two of us walked to Tanners house just up the block. It made sense why he was always at the corner store, he lived close. His house was rusty baby blue, with paint slowly chipping off in scattered areas. Underneath the hue of blue was white paint that previously ruled the house. A small chain-link fence circled the house, it was clearly made for only small animals. The fence was only around four feet in height with every other link rusted raw. The lawn was well kept and vibrant for the most part though.

Tanner's windows were barred shut around the building. His closest neighbor was a block away. He was fortunate enough to live next to an alleyway on the west side of his house & the east scrapped against an abandoned building. Tanner explained that he lived in the house since he was born. His grandfather bought the house in his youth and passed it down. When his parents retired they moved to Miami, leaving him the house. He invited me in to talk and so I could wash up, I was pretty dirty at the time.

Tanner started to unlock an almost infinite number of locks on the door. I tried my best not to laugh at the ridiculous number of locks he had. It was quite comical though; even in the world's most dangerous city, who the hell needs that many locks?

I walked into the warm dark house with low expectations. Tanner flipped a few switches to illuminate the house. He messed with the thermostat to cool down the temperature. The interior was nothing like I imagined. The floors were polished wood, complimenting white walls in an open surrounding. The room to the left was an inviting living room with a giant leather plush couches. The room adjacent to it held a billiards table and an entertainment center. There were family photos on the walls, as well as paintings.   I was quite taken back by how immaculate the house was and felt out of place. I was filthy and covered in blood, also in great need of a shower. Luckily, it was clear Tanner showed his gratitude through his hospitality.

"There is a bathroom right through the hall, second door on your right, and there is one in the den right there."

"Alright thanks man, I'll be right out."

I proceeded through the den to feed my curiosity of the house. The den had an entertainment center with gaming systems and bean bag seats. It had an emo teen feeling to it, the walls had posters instead of paintings. Next to the television rested a two foot long weed bong ready to go. I washed off my face in the bathroom sink and glanced into the mirror. Who am I? Who am I becoming, fighting with strangers? I heard a slight knock on the door, it was Tanner. He was holding a stack of clothes, a towel and two straight billed hats.

"Hey man I brought you something."

"What's all this?"

"I don't know what size you wear, but there's a couple sizes for you to choose from in here. You are welcome to take a shower if you need to, the lock on the door works if you think it's weird. Oh and I like wearing a hat, I don't know about you but have your pick."

I didn't quite know what to say.

"Thanks man, that's really nice of you. I really appreciate it."

"Nah man, don't mention it."

After a quick shower, I changed into the only large clothes he had. I wore a white shirt with a symbol for New York on the front. I liked a black hat with a large capital "B" stitched in white. To be honest I didn't wear hats, but I thought the gesture was sweet so I wore one.

I brought back the remaining clothes back to him in the living room. He jumped up in excitement pointing at the hat.

"I thought you might like that one, it's yours, keep it. The clothes too."

He took the left over pile and set it down on a couch.

"Thank you!"

"Don't mention it, can I get you a beer or something to drink?"

"Not much of a beer drinker, but after a day like today what the hell."

He knew that I was underage, so my comment felt stupid after I said it aloud.

Tanner went to grab some beer from the fridge. I was negligent to tell him that it would be my first beer ever. Tried beer before and even held it at parties, but this was to give the illusion of drinking. I expected to be brought a regular size beer bottle that I could then baby-sit until leaving. Instead a massive forty ounce beer was placed in front of me inside a paper sack. I slid the opened beer from the brown paper sheath.

"That's 'Mad Dog', here you're either 'Mickey's' or 'Mad Dog' Witch one are you?"

"Oh, Mad Dog.' For sure, always 'Mad Dog' forget 'Mickey's'"

Tanner started laughing. I wasn't sure if he was laughing because he saw through my lie, or he thought I was trying to be funny. Either way, his laugh was contagious. Tanner plopped down on a couch and told me to have a seat.

We sat in silence for a while drinking before anything was said. Tanner set his bottle down on a cherry coffee table, he removed the paper bag & belched. I was amazed to see that the beer was empty, who could drink that fast? My beer was missing an ounce at most, leaving me thirty-nine to go. He offered me another beer as he returned to the kitchen. I told him that I was still working on the one I had, which was an understatement.

Tanner shouted from the kitchen,

"Thanks for the help man! If you hadn't come I would have been screwed. Just don't understand why you came though, don't get me wrong I appreciate it, but what the hell were you thinking? Do you just go around saving people all day or what?"

Tanner returned to the living room holding two more forty once beers. He probably knew that I a ton left, but looking back I understand. This was Tanner's way of saying that I should stay a while.

"What like a super hero? Oh yeah that's funny. Nah man it's not like that, I just saw that you could have ran but fought instead. I admire that. Also, I didn't know that you were a freaking black belt in Karate."

He began laughing hysterically.

"No, no I kind of do this for a living."

"You are a boxer for a living?"

"Kind of."

"You're a fighter for a living?"

"Kind of." He said again.

"Are you going to tell me what you do for a living?"

"Maybe, only time will tell."

"Well, anyways I wanted to help because I saw you that day."

"What day?"

"When you paid for the groceries we took at the corner store."

"That was you?"

"Yeah and my brother and sister."

"Oh, that pregnant girl is your sister?"

"What? Oh no, she's not really pregnant. She did that to get groceries."

"Damn dude, that's some kind of hustle! I like it, totally fell for it by the way. Like, that was the reason I paid for her stuff. To be honest I felt bad for her bro, didn't really notice you and your brother."

"No you don't understand, it wasn't a hustle. We were just hungry."

"Look I get it, but was she pregnant?"

"No."

"Did you guys work together?"

"Of course."

"Did you get something for nothing?"

"Well, yeah." I said baffled.

"That's literally the definition of a hustle. Not hatting on it, I'm just saying that what you did was straight hustling."

"Oh, well I never thought about it like that."

Tanner had a face of approval, I did not argue with him and he liked that about me.

"Look really there are only two kinds of people. Those that hustle and those who get hustled. Now I'm not talking about crime necessarily, I'm talking about drive. The thing that motivates you to rise to the top, when everyone else follows. You're different Brian, I like that about you."

"Thanks, but it's not intentional."

"Well either way, you make sense to me. And again, thank you."

"Cheers!" I saluted his gratitude.

He was so taken back by me, he wanted to know everything about me. So I told him about the past week. That alone held enough information about me to explain why I was there. One sentence was all I truly needed to tell the story.

"Dad got hurt, we fled to our uncle, survived until resources ran out."

I like to keep things short. Though to be honest, it took about forty five minutes trying to tell the full story. Tanner kept interrupting to ask question after question. I would have probably done the same thing in that situation. All of my answers to his questions were brief and ambiguous though. After all he was a stranger to me, we shared the fight and charity for Christy. But at the end of the day, he still had to earn my trust. There was so little I knew, I had some questions of my own.

"So, what were those guys mad at you for in the first place? I mean that one guy really didn't like you."

"Well, it's kind of a crazy story; I actually know all of those guys who jumped me. Especially the main guy yelling at me, I used to party with him all the time."

"Really?"

"Yeah, his boys tagged along from time to time and I did business with a few of them on more than one occasion."

"I'm not even going to ask."

"Well let's just say when someone needs something, they go to me."

"Fair enough."

"Anyways the main guy they call eight-ball. He is the leader of the group we fought."

"So they really call that guy eight-ball?"

"Yeah, like his tattoo."

"I thought that his name might be eight-ball, like for selling coke."

"Well that's probably why he got the tattoo."

I started to realize that I was interrupting Tanner as-much-as he was earlier. It could be due to mimicry for approval, like I wanted to be friends.

"Sorry, I'll let you finish."

"No worries, so anyways like I was saying. That group runs low grade blow east of here, making eight-ball think he is some drug kingpin or something. He and all his little homo friends are pussies if you ask me, but that has nothing to do with this."

"I think we are getting off topic bro." I

"Right, anyways last week I had a party and it got pretty out of control. Ended up in bed with some fat chick and her hot friend. It was a two for one deal, which kind of sucked because I'm not one for big girls. Trust me this other girl was hot though! I mean great tits, a nice ass, perfect. Figured she was worth taking the bullet on the side bang if you know what I mean. So we start going at it. We did double doggie style, but it was like a poodle and a St. Bernard."

His tone of voice had me in tears laughing. The alcohol definitely had an effect on the volume of my laughter and he was starting to notice.

Tanner Continued.

"So we do our thing and I wake up the next morning to some fighting outside. So I looked and the girls from last night were fighting with Eight Ball. So, naturally I grab my piece, walk outside and yell 'Yo! What the fuck is going on?' He gets all hurt, crying and shit. It turns out the fat chick was his sister and the hot one was his girl!"

"D-a-m-n!" I yelled.

"Well, long story short he tried to fight me right then and there, but I pointed my piece at him and it was all over."

"So if you keep a gun on you? Then why didn't you end it quickly when those guys came after you?"

"Good question, today I was rolling with Craze and Texas. They were the two guys you saw with me. We were supposed to meet up with some girls down the street so I left my piece. When they took off running it was obvious it was a set up. Would've been beaten to death, but you showed up and now we're here."

He looked at me as if he owed a life debt.

"Thanks again man, I won't soon forget this."

"Don't mention it, my pleasure." I said.

The booze was starting to get to me, I was slightly dizzy. I told Tanner that I needed to leave, he insisted on giving me a ride. I argued that he had just drank two forty ounce beers and probably should not drive. Thus he insisted on walking me home instead, it was hard to tell him no. Also I did not mind the company for a change.

We strolled to the train yard late from the time I promised. Vince and Christy were probably worried sick for me. We were supposed to meet back up, I didn't think about them. What if something happened to them while I was away? Not only did I come back empty handed, but also beat-up, with a stranger.

Tanner was aware that we were living in an abandoned train, but I still felt ashamed. I'm not quite sure the reason, it just felt that way. My mother could relate to company coming over with a dirty house. It was the principal, it didn't define us.

Eventually I had metabolized all the alcohol during the walk. I was still rambling on about my mother. Tanner just listened for the most part, which was nice. He was different from others who spoke to me like I were a child. Respectfully I've been the same person since I was thirteen. Not too much changed about my personality, or the way I think. I'm glad he saw me as an equal.

Tanner was an only child and his parents were wealthy. They owned several properties, but Tanner said he makes his own money. Such circumstances are hard to believe, though I was beginning to trust him.

Our journey came to a close as we neared the old train yard. The day had come to a screeching-halt after trumping the excitement from the day. I made a friend and gained several enemies.

A moment came that I was not expecting. When I was saying my good-byes to Tanner, he stunned me. He had a genuine look of dismay, he was worried. It could have been a father instinct inside of him. Whatever it was made Tanner linger as I jumped over the fence.

We need each other

Christy and Vince heard the noise from the fence, as I thrusted upward to advance over. They peaked their faces out of the train cart. Christy noticed Tanner at the Fence and their eyes locked. Tanner waved at her to break the tension, she waved back. Though she was curious why I was with him. Vince held contention in his heart that I was late & with a stranger. Who could blame him? It was a drastic thing to do on my part.

I heard Tanners voice over my shoulder as I walked to the train.

"Yo! You guys hungry? I'm ordering pizza!" Tanner shouted.

Vince ran out of the train cart before I could introduce the strange man. Christy shortly then after chasing Vince shouting "He said pizza!"

My stomach was full of beer, so I had forgotten that my siblings were starving.

Tanner introduced himself after everyone got over the fence. He was very kind for feeding us, he had my respect for another reason once again. Why was this guy so nice to us? Was it pity, or appreciation for aid? Perhaps a mix of the two, after seeing the state of some teenagers trying to survive.

Tanner and Vince connected almost instantly. They were an odd pair, like they were the same person separated by a decade. Vince and Tanner walked ahead talking about nonsensical jargon, after the initial introduction questions. Who are you? How do you know my brother? What kind of necklace is that? Vince had a way of asking important inquiries while questioning fashion. Tanner was straight to the point each time he was interrogated.

It became easy for Vince to pry information quickly. They walked ahead of me while Christy stuck to my side. She informed me that they had begged on the corner for an hour and made forty dollars. Then they stayed another three or four hours without making a dime. My siblings returned to the train waiting for me to return with the forty.

Christy was excited that they had money for dinner already. She said that it felt like our luck was changing. We had finally hit rock bottom, so we could finally move in the other direction. Christy told me that she prayed for me to come back safe. Shortly after that, I arrived beaten-up with a complete stranger. Once Vince approved, she knew things were good.

Christy was becoming a savage little person as well. She informed me that she lingered behind in-case Tanner tried to start trouble. She was carrying the six shooter pistol under a ratty dark grey sweater she wore. Vince knew she had the gun, they were little evil geniuses.

I had earned no money in the time I was gone, coming back empty again. I saw luck going in the wrong direction, but Christy had a way of looking on the positives of things. She envisioned going to beg at the same spot every day at the same time. She would take Vince and come back. After a week or so, we could afford a ticket home.

For some reason my mind was somewhere else. My father still in the hospital and I'm making friends. The guilt was clawing at me for having fun. We were still just surviving, but it was fun. It felt like we were outlaws, living in the wild-west, taking what we wanted. We had protection in ourselves, as well as lethal force. Nothing was going to stop us but life itself. Yet I felt a great deal of grief. I did miss my life back home, but that's not what waited for us. We would return to a manhunt with my name on it. Could I be charged with kidnaping? I was paranoid of the consequences, but it quickly slipped away.

The moment I was living in was blissful. Finally a time where we all thought about dinner, not running or surviving. Vince was rambling on about the pizza as if he knew the area, or was going to suggest a place. Tanner ended up ordering three large pizzas. Enough to feed a rather large family. We all ate at the table as if we were one. I was going to solve the Tanner mystery after eating my favorite meal. It was good pizza too! There wasn't a single slice left when we were done.

The television blared the across Tanners house. My little brother Vince made himself perfectly comfortable after dinner. Tanner told him he could watch TV after dinner and Vince took full advantage.

My little brother tried to read people by seeing what channels they had. If they were sports fanatics then everything was likely to be sports, nothing else. Vince loved women with cats, they were more likely to have every channel possible. Tanner had an impressive list by my brother's standards. He was accompanied by Christie who simply enjoyed stretching out on the couches.

I played a game of billiards in the next room with Tanner. It was weird being in this house twice in one day. Almost as if I knew him my whole life.

"Come on, let me know what's on your mind kid." Tanner said. He re-raked the balls and dusted his pool stick.

"Nothing I appreciate everything, the food, the hospitality. I get that you're a good guy, but I still don't understand why you invited us back?"

"It's pretty simple Brian, I had a change of heart last second. We can help each other, you need me."

"I don't need anyone." I said defensively.

"Sorry, don't take me the wrong way. I mean I can help you, and you can help me."

"How so?"

"Well for starters, I think that we can find your grandfather."

Tanner lined up the cue ball and sunk three balls from the break.

"You're solids."

"You can find my grandpa?"

"Well, it dawned on me that if you really were the grandson of a mob boss, then maybe you could talk to him for me."

"About what?"

"Remember how I said my parents were rich and away?"

"Yeah."

"That was a bit of a stretch, they went to prison for embezzlement. All of their assets were frozen and I've been saving for a lawyer to fight the case. If we find your grandfather then maybe he can help me."

"Hmm, but how would you find him." I questioned.

"Oh, well that part is easy. You know his name, and I know most of the top guys around here. I'll just ask around."

"I already asked around." I exclaimed.

"Yeah, but you didn't ask the right people."

I was not much of a pool player, I scratched my first shot. Tanner went on to sink in another two balls before missing. His movements were smooth, the balls did not make a sound. They just slid across the table, ever so slightly. When I set up my shot, I used my shoulders to push into the balls. Noise erupted into the room, bleeding over the television. It was a bit dramatic, but oh how powerful I felt.

"So what if we don't find grandpa or uncle Vinny?"

"That is the second part of my offer, we can still help each other. You need somewhere to stay while you get on your feet right?"

"Of course."

"My parents are locked up, I'm all alone here. Thought maybe the three of you could bunk in the basement. You would have your own bathroom while you stay here."

"What would we have to do in return?"

"Well your brother and sister can just chill all day, they don't need to do anything."

"What about me?"

"To be honest Brian, I need fighters. Two of them to be exact. The same two that ran away today, leaving me behind. They actually fight for me."

He missed when setting up his next shot at the billiards game. Possibly because he knew how bad I was at the pool, I needed all the help I could get. Even if he was cheating in my favor.

"So I got to know man, what exactly do you do? I mean I'm not doing so well on money right now."

"I need someone I can trust Brian."

"And you want me to fight for you?"

"Um, yes."

"And Vince, Christie and I stay in the basement?"

"Uh huh." He nodded.

"No strings attached?"

"Right; wait, no, with strings-attached. I'm saying you fighting is the strings we are talking about. Or getting your grandfather to help me. Either way, we both win."

"Bare knuckle?"

"No, we actually have gloves and timed matches. It's legit."

I took my time thinking while taking my turn on the table. My next shots had to be perfect! Instantly the game was over because I sunk the wrong ball. Tanner was quick to notice.

"Oh that eight ball will get you if you're not watching for it. Sorry bud, better luck next time."

Was not quite sure if he was patronizing me or not. I lost the game, but agreed to the terms.

"Okay, let's do it."

"Really? Great, we are going to make a great team."

"So you'll help me find slick?"

"Of course, I'll start that right away."

"Really? Awesome! My grandfather's full name is Ignacio Rodriguez Vega, everyone calls him Slick or Big Slick. My uncle's name is Vincent just like my brother."

"Thought you guys were Italian?"

"We are, my grandpa slick is half Italian and half Mexican."

"Then why the hell is your sister white?"

"Oh, my mom is full blooded Irish."

"So you're Mexican, Italian, and Irish?"

"Yup!"

"Sheesh! Thought my family was crazy, why is your grandpa called Slick?"

"Not quite sure, he's had that nickname forever."

"Cool, how hard could it be to find them right?"

"So you don't know them in your line of work?"

"About that, I'm more of an entrepreneurial kind of guy and less of a drug dealer. That doesn't mean that we can't find them though. I know who most of the sellers around here."

"It's a deal then, either way I'll fight. When do we start?"

"We have fight night this weekend. Start training immediately. As for me, tomorrow the man hunt starts for your grandpa."

"Do you know who I would fight?"

"It changes weekly, depends mostly on the outcome of who shows up. Really it's all random, we need you in case of an odd number. Most of the guys are pretty small, you'll be fine." He assured me.

"So anyone can fight?"

"Yeah, might as well just explain it now. So every other Saturday I set up a 'fight night.' Tournament style boxing with gloves, one hundred dollars to enter. Second place gets double their buy-in, winner takes the rest."

"So, what's in it for you if the fighters make all the money?" I grilled.

"Good question, for me it's the side action. People place bets with the house on who will win each fight. If the house wins, then I win. Does that make sense?"

"Yes."

"Oh, and another thing. I make money at the door for entrance as well as sell beer. By the end of the night everyone is happy."

"Everyone? Even the losers?"

"Yes everyone, unlike most people I don't get too greedy. People have a good time coming to my events. There are people who just want to see a fight, those who love gambling, and fighters who only want to fight."

Tanner seemed to be quite proud of what he had built. It was a small illegal gambling ring, I understood the concept. There were still far too many questions that I had for him. Instead I remained quiet and allowed him to finish.

"That's why earlier I said that fighting is 'kind of' what I do for a living. Believe it or not I fight once a month at least, but just for fun."

"You're crazy, but I like it. You want to play another game?"

"Nah, let's go into the kitchen and go over some details. Want a beer?"

"Sure, sounds good." I said, but what I meant to say was: "Hell no it tastes fucking horrible."

Vince and Christie could hear most of what we talked about, there was no getting around it being in the billiards room. They didn't say a word, letting me do the talking. Maybe to see what I can do, making the decisions for the house. We moved to the kitchen while my siblings sprawled out on the couches. I'm sure that it was a paradise in itself.

Tanner and I ended up talking for hours. Beer was the equivalent to drinking coffee late at night with a distant family member. My father would love drinking coffee in the evening (freaking psycho!). For me coming into adulthood beer seemed to be the best resource to relate.

I theorize that you need a symbolic drink to gap the awkward silence of most conversations. Ritualistic in nature, a shared beverage builds relationships. Even in the movies you'll hear "*Want to grab a drink?*" or "*Let's get some coffee.*" This signifies, "I want to get to know you better." Just like any beverage, one drink leads to another, opening the lines of communication and nostalgia for the dialogue. Needless to say we shared multiple drinks, while embellishing on our lives.

Tanner started fight night out of his home a year ago. The idea was quite brilliant. He had a pair of boxing gloves hanging on his wall, above some family photos. His father was a boxer early on in his life, going pretty far. He taught Tanner how to fight as a kid for bonding time. It was a memory he held close to his heart.

One night Tanner threw a party at his house, a really large one. A few of the people noticed the boxing gloves and talked about how they used to box. Words were exchanged on style and structure, and eventually challenges were made. Tanner being ballsy fought first, he led the party to his basement were the damage would be contained. Away from the valuables and breakables, ironically where we are staying. He went for three fights that night, putting on a show. People started taking side action on who would win each bout. After the fight another pair wanted to have a go. From there Tanner realized that he had something people wanted to be part of. A modern day *Fight Club*, but without the multiple personality disorder.

At the time he had a grow operation for marijuana. He sold weed and lots of it, but the risk was high. In one evening at fight night Tanner made a thousand dollars. That was a significant difference. Plus the risk seemed worth it for the thrill.

What he was doing was legal in Vegas. The boxing matches were timed and regulated by a referee. People came for the excitement alone, just being part of something illegal. He said that the feeling was better than ecstasy, I never tried it, and so I had to take his word on that. As his project grew, so did the venue. Tanner scouted new locations for every fight night. He would literally stake out an abandoned business for weeks to know everything about it.

He wanted to know who came, who left and every time there was a siren. When a location was finally chosen, there was a mass text stating *"It's on!"*

Then there was a password to get into the spot with security. Lastly, the boxing site was texted an hour before the actual fights began. Hundreds showed from all over the city, it gave him a true feeling of accomplishment. Tanner saw a business, to him it had all the functions of a business with different downfalls. He had employees, vendors, supply-and-demand, as well as stable income. He ran security with one guy. Tanner said the man was six foot five, three hundred and fifty pounds. Everything normally ran smooth as silk, he only ever had one instance where his body guard stepped in. It was over a jealous husband of one of the ring girls. He sat in the crowd and heard some guys talking about her. Easy to see an altercation happening there, so Tanner only hired single ring girls after that.

Fight night was exciting to me, I was not a fighter by any means. But within the year my number of unintentional disputes were climbing anyways. For some reason, the lifestyle called to me. I wanted to be part of the Tanner Brady roller-coaster. In the end I would either find my lost family or support the family I had. My father would not be proud of my decisions, but could he judge me? I was only doing what was needed to survive. Truly there was a desire in my heart to be a bigger picture sort of guy. Fight night seemed like an opportunity to invest, something that could grow into a legitimate business.

After another round of booze, Tanner came clean on his parents and his entire situation.

It could have been the beer talking, but he became brutally honest. His parents owned and managed properties all over the country for their company. When his father was charged for embezzlement he fled, with his wife to Colorado. Tanner's mother was officially the Vice President of their company.

Though she did mostly advertisement and had little to do with the crime. His parents were caught and charged in Colorado, during a speed trap. The entirety of their empire was taken except for the house. The judge set a bail for one million each. Tanner was forced to put up the house along with cash for a bondsman to bail out his parents. Just as they were released, again they left the state and were caught, yet again. Now with a bail of five million each.

Tanner explained that he was fighting to keep the house and pay the bondsman. He had court fees, lawyer costs, and the mortgage.

It was no wonder why he needed so much income to survive and still live in the ghetto. He orchestrated illicit activities in a grand scale to fight for his parents. My crimes were petty and avoidable for the most part.

As Tanner continued he explained that the true concern was for his mother. He wanted to get her out of jail, she hated everything about the place. When he saw me fight, he thought of opportunity; but after I told him of my mobster family, Tanner saw me as a Godsend.

It became clear during our gathering that I was a golden goose to him, but it did not bother me. Instead it provided me shelter from the cold and food for my family. After all I too was running from something and needed a crutch. Fortune happened to be on my side, this man truly wanted to find my family. He was the only person that could locate them as well.

Tanner explained the territory layout which was surprisingly simple, yet fascinating. There were gangs, but that's what they were to him. Just small groups of people lingering.

 He bellowed that the local gangs were "Small time" They only bother outsiders, i.e. myself. They own block corners if that, very small space to constantly inhabit. The local gangs answer to suppliers who aren't exclusive. If you bought from them or knew them then you had the "Hook-up" An all-access pass to a large scale supplier. They were considered to own the block being local, each with a small army. Mess with a supplier and you'll never be found. Eight ball, the guy I low-bowed in the groin, was a supplier. (Apparently that meant being marked for death.) Tanner was a local entertainer of sorts so he lived in a grey area. No one messed with the entertainment out of fear of losing jester.

Above the supplier were traffickers, they moved product across borders on state or international level. Rarely local and often unknown to most. They had cartels and actual armies at their disposal. Normally dealing with hired assassins if need be.

Tanner thought that my grandfather might be a trafficker, he only knew of one and has never seen him. Tanner said that he heard ghost stories about a guy named "Graveyard" or "Grave Digger" Depending on who tells the story. Apparently the guy is currently still in prison, but runs things in KC in silence. Tanner says that those who cross wrongful paths with the "Grave Digger" End up digging their own grave. Refuse and your family digs extra holes that day. Tanner said he was middle-aged, so there was no way that guy could be my grandfather,

He knew nobody with my relative's names, but maybe the suppliers knew something. He did know most of them and happened to be one. Tanner supplied homegrown marijuana, he was very proud of the product.

"Made right here in the U.S.A." Tanner remarked.

To him the grow operation was small, but he still supplied. A warrant would all but seal his fate as the grow-op was in the house. He had a secret ladder that was sealed into the attic. When exposed, it led to a homemade hydroponic system. In total tanner had six plants, he rotated in blooming cycles of two. Each month two plants were ready to dry, then they dried for six weeks. Tanner said that the process gave him around two pounds a month. The street value was seven thousand or higher. He explained that the cost was high for two reasons: One, Tanner grew in an extremely illegal state for marijuana. Growers were getting prison time in Kansas vs. heath benefits in California with a license. The second reason was that most weed came from Mexico. Tanner's product was exclusive to the block for buyers and grown with care in-doors. Tanner said that the value of his weed went up as the amount sold lowered. Meaning the guys doing the foot work had room for profit.

His weed was known as "Indo-Hydro-Chronic" and the name of his personal strain was "Bogart" He exclaimed for the actor, but I was unaware of his reasoning for most things. It was a "*How-to: The Streets*" novel worth of information in a drunken night. Similar to the culture shock of traveling abroad, I was living in a place I did not understand.

Tanners golden rule of the game was simple "Never get greedy" he argued that he only made a little over two hundred an ounce and normally sold ninety percent in bulk.

"After drying the bud, it's gone, fast bro!" Tanner exclaimed.

To him this was his way of keeping his hands out of the cookie jar. Tanner had the product sold before he could get caught, or so he thought.

He explained that per gram held the true value of the marijuana, the person who received the most for a single gram earned highest. For twenty dollars a gram the product was worth close to nine thousand dollars a pound. Tanner was selling the same pound for more than half of the street value. He was a grower, truly he controlled the local home grown market.

There was a recent drought, when it was hard to get low grade Mexican bud or high grade. He alleged that the prices were nearly double at forty to fifty dollars for a single gram of high grade weed. To him that was outrageous, but elsewhere people were scammed for higher.

His life was laid out before my eyes, fully transparent. I learned his past, present and even future aspirations. It seemed only right that I divulge further information about myself. Whether or not it was a good decision, I felt like I knew the guy.

"To me, school was boring. I excelled tremendously, but still had no desire to go to college. This was the secret that I kept from my father."

"You talk like a narrator a little Brian, have you ever been told that before?"

"Uh, no I suppose not."

Tanner laughed rambunctiously. "See, like right there, you're super proper. It's not a bad thing, it's just easy to spot you as an outsider."

"Damn really?"

"Yeah dude, don't take this the wrong way but you sound white as hell."

"Well, I am white. I mean half white, but it's full Irish."

"People don't care about your genealogy Brian, they judge you based on your appearance and speech." He explained.

"So you judge me as white?"

"Nah, the opposite, I expect Cholo when seeing you, but get Carlton instead."

"Ouch! What did I do?"

"Sorry, don't mind me. I'm just clowning dog! Continue, so what did you want to do if not college?"

He seemed sincere and it felt like his sense of humor was observational like Vince. Probably why they reminded me of one another. I told Tanner the truth

"As a child I wanted to be a film Director, cameras fascinated me. Great stories were hard to come by, I wanted to only tell captivating tales."

"Why were good stories hard to come by?"

"Think about how many movies you have watched vs. how many you could watch every day."

"Damn, true. So what separates the two?"

"Characters that make the audience feel empathy."

"Like you know them?"

"Basically, it's like the audience sees themselves in the character. The right story can be life changing."

Tanner was skeptical. "No movie has ever changed my life bro, I get the thing about your passion, but give me one example."

"Sure, have you ever seen a movie about a boxer who rises from nothing?"

"Of course."

"Imagine how many people take up boxing after watching that."

"Shit! That's deep bro, you should have gone into psychology." Tanner said.

"Not for me, I just love good stories. They change me sometimes."

"Dude! You should be a writer! You could write my story, there is some weird shit in there."

"Well I think that school is closed for me after assaulting a cop. I was homeless just hours ago."

Tanner patted me on the back.

"You're doing well for yourself Brian. Don't let go of those dreams just yet. This is just a chapter of your story."

He left me with that wisdom and retreated to bed.

The basement looked nothing like a basement. It was completely finished from top to bottom. The downstairs had its own shower, something Christy appreciated. There were two rooms, both with queen sized beds. For a moment it was like we were visiting our uncle. Still less then twenty-four hours had passed before meeting Tanner. Thus we slept all in one room, I gave Vince and Christie the bed. For myself the floor was better than the train, I was thankful for the roof over my head.

Staring at the white speckled ceiling in Tanners basement I assembled a plan. Tomorrow would be a special day, and it was time to start training. Sleep greeted me with open arms.

The next morning I awoke to an empty room. I assumed the worst and rushed upstairs. Vince was playing video games and Christy was baking cookies. I had to pinch myself to make sure I was awake. We were in a bizarre version of our own house. Tanner told my siblings to make themselves at home, he gave my sister a tour of the kitchen and off he went. My guard lowered, maybe God was looking after us.

It was time for me to hop-to and take care of some business as well, unknown to everyone else. After showering and a quick breakfast I asked Christy for the money she earned begging. It took some convincing, but she gave it to me. I also argued with Vince a bit before leaving. He didn't understand the importance of my sudden absence. It was my fault however, that information wasn't for him. He would probably advise me against it anyways. My siblings felt safer if I took the pistol.

So I left the house with forty-two dollars and a pistol. There was a bag in the motel we stayed in, I had to retrieve it. Tanner could empty the bag fast, based on his weed knowledge. Hopefully no one had found my hiding place.

Tanner's house was close to the corner store, only blocks from the motel we stayed. It was an easy task I assumed.

I started to jog to the motel with a plan to knock on the door first, and ask nicely to use the restroom. With my luck I the room would be empty and I'd have to barter with the owner. I knocked on the motel door out of breath. A man answered the door casually dressed holding a coffee mug.

"Hello sir, sorry to be blunt. I'm going to shit my pants if I can't get to a bathroom soon. I'll give you twenty dollars for five minutes. Please, I'm dying." I said while holding my rear.

"Yeah, sure." The man said.

I rushed in the door without a moment to spare and into the bathroom.

"Hey, you better not make a mess in there. Leave the fan on too!" Said the man through the door.

I flushed the toilet to sell the odd occurrence while rapidly tearing the bag from the ceiling and empting its content into my pockets. Within a sixty seconds of entering I had everything and proceeded to pay the man.

"Thank you sir! Left the fan on, flushed twice." I said fleeing.

"Yeah, quick twenty right?"

"Most expensive dump I ever took."

I was back to Tanners house in the blink of an eye.

"You're back already?" Vince said.

"Yeah, it was quick. Hey do you want to talk a bit?"

"Sure."

My brother continued into the game room, I followed closely behind.

"You cool?"

"Always."

"You don't feel cool, you sure?"

Vince continued his video game that he had paused. His attention was mostly focused on the television, it was hard to competing with a game.

"Everything is fine, just enjoying the moment."

"What moment? This one?"

"Yes actually, who knows where the hell we'll be next. Might as well enjoy the flat-screen and hot food." His tone changed to sarcastic.

The notion was relatable after what we went through, stability was a dream.

"Okay, well I love you little brother. I'm here if you need me, hopefully we go home soon."

"Love you too, you think we will leave soon?"

"Maybe, I think that Tanner has a real shot at finding grandpa. That's all we need and everything will be better."

"Everything?"

"Not everything exactly, but he can take custody so we aren't split up. He might be able to get me out of trouble as well."

Vince was not too convinced about the last part, grandpa was just an old man to him.

"Sounds great Brian, let me know when you find him."

I sighed and walked away, Vince was revealing my false hope. We didn't know my grandfather very well, so I couldn't comment on his ability to save us. There was a chance that he didn't give a damn about us. Maybe my father didn't keep him away, but Slick just never visited.

The kitchen had a brighter side to things, my sister was washing the dishes. The kitchen was large with wide counter tops and a center island. Atop the isle was a plate full of brownish plain cookies. I tried one thinking it was peanut butter, it tasted like butterscotch instead. The delicious treats melted in my mouth with a fragrant maple sent. Immediately I had a second cookie.

"Christy these are amazing! What did you put in them?"

"Thanks, they are kind of thrown together really." She replied.

I giggled, how humble. "Whatever these things are really freaking good. What are they?"

"Hard to explain what they are. I wanted to make chocolate chip cookies, but have no chocolate chips. No sugar, flour, milk or eggs either."

"How the heck did you make them then?"

My sister laughed explaining her creation.

"Tanner had a bran muffin mix, so I used that. Thought, hmm, 'This is going to be terrible' so put in some sweetened condensed milk. The batter tasted like biscuits and was too thick. So then I put in maple syrup. Then the batter was too runny so I threw in a few packs of butterscotch pudding mix."

"Well they are definitely unique." I reached for another cookie.

"Thanks, maybe we should keep the recipe then."

"For sure, call it Christy cookies."

"If I were to name a cookie after me, it wouldn't be called Christy cookies Brian."

"Well sorry, Miss Thang. What would you call them then?" I smiled.

"They would be real cookies for one and they would be called Canadian Whiskey treats."

The name was hilarious to me because I was corrected after naming the cookie. At least the name I created made sense.

"I don't get it."

My sister smiled at me, she couldn't keep a poker face while telling a joke.

"Because the maple syrup and butterscotch." dumbfounded.

"Oh maple, scotch. Canadian, Scottish."

"And they both make whiskey."

"Did you just come up with that stupid, but extremely well layered name just now?"

"Yeah."

We both shared in an uncontrollable nervous laughter. This girl had intellectual superpowers. I didn't know how she became so quick witted. I loved my siblings, but there were times that it felt like we were strangers. I flicked her thick curly hair back and forth lovingly.

"Why do you know cookies so well?"

"Because of mom." She said.

"Really?"

"Yeah you might be the Chef in the family Brian, but I'm the baker."

"I'm fine with that, but I just like to cook some things. How do you know cookies if you never technically met mom?"

"Because she had tons of baking books and wrote notes in all of them, it's how I 'feel her spirt."

She smiled and flicked her hair back away from me. For a second I saw my mother's face during her hair toss. As if my mother was agreeing with her, showing me she was with Christy.

"I can remember something she said when I ran in the kitchen one day."

"What's that?"

"She always said 'Cookie are for everyone, but only we get the dough.'"

My sister teared up, clinching her arms tightly around me.

"I just want to know her Brian, she died because of me." Christy proceeded crying.

"Hey don't do that do yourself babe. She died to save you, not because of you."

"Why am I so special? If she let me die, then you'd have a mom now."

"Look sis, we never lost mom. You were right when you said her spirit is with you. More than that, you are the spitting image of her. If you want to know mom then look in the mirror. Look what she gave her life to protect."

Christy wiped the tears from her eyes and smiled.

"Brian, I'm not scared anymore, I know you'll protect us like mom did. I love you." Christy continued sobbing.

"I love you too sis, we will get through this, I promise. As long as we stick together.

It was a false promise, I was just as uncertain as she was. But it was my job to hide those emotions from her. That's what an older brother should do, keep my sister composed.

Fight Night

"Great news! I've got great news!" Tanner said coming home through the back door of the house. He saw the plate full of cookies and went for one, after just one bite he grabbed three more. "These are dope cookies by the way!"

"What's the news?" I asked Tanner.

"Might have found your grandfather."

"Already?"

"Woah, you're good." Said Christy

"Eh, I try. Get this B, word got out about the Vega name. Someone was representing the Vega boss just the other day."

"Yeah, that was me."

"For real?" Tanner asked suspiciously.

"Seriously, I actually wanted to talk to you in private about something."

"Sure, we can go to my room."

"Hold the phone, tell me! Did you find grandpa or not?" Christy yelled at we exited the room.

"Maybe, we will have more info tonight." Tanner yelled back to keep her at bay.

Tanner led me up the stairs to his bedroom. The master suit was arguably bigger than his living room. It took up an entire floor excluding a laundry room and small storage room. I came clean with everything and we had no beer this time. My pockets were still full of drugs, so I gave it to him. Then I showed him my pistol facing downward, so he would not be alarmed. Tanner informed me that the bags were full of heroin. He told me that it was best to get rid of the drugs and gun quick. Since people know about the Vega name, Tanner convinced me to take on an alias. He said I should pick something that was personal, so it was easy to answer to. I chose Ox as my nickname, it was rightfully given to me by my mother & father. It was destiny.

"We have a clue who your grandpa is."

"That's awesome, what is it?"

"Well, we are still waiting to hear back in full, but I reached out to the inside."

"What does that mean exactly?"

"It means that I talked to my connections in prison. People know the name Slick on the inside. He used to be big time, who knows how much he is actually worth. The guy might be a kingpin for all we know."

"So we can find him?"

"Not quite, people like that aren't just found. You have to put word out that you are looking first."

"Then what?"

"Then he finds you."

Tanner told me not to worry about the gang, what they had was probably stolen anyways. For my honesty Tanner promised to sell the loot and give me fifty percent. He made some phone calls and we waited downstairs.

Vice was asked to take the gaming system to the basement with Christy. He was happy to be left out for once, Vince was too into his games to care. I didn't want them being exposed to hard drugs, really that was the only concern. Christy took a nap while my brother took a holiday. Suddenly two guys walk into Tanners house arguing, both of them did not notice that I was sitting on the couch. I already knew their names, Lance and Spanish. Tanner used them frequently and paid generously for the discrete work.

"What do you mean? How is an ostrich not a bird?" Lance argued.

"I'm telling you! Think about it, them fools can't fly. Ostriches only have feathers." Spanish replied.

"Hell nah, how you know they can't fly? You ever seen a freaking Ostrich?"

"Yes as a matter of fact, saw them at the zoo. I know things."

"Please you don't know nothing, next you'll tell me that a turkey isn't a bird either."

"You ever seen a turkey fly Lance?"

"Are you kidding me? Bat's fly, that don't mean they're birds."

"YO! Do y'all want to shut the hell up for a second?" Tanner raised his voice.

"My bad." Lance said putting his head down.

"Yeah my fault dog. Who are you?" Spanish asked looking at me.

"This is my boy Brian, show some respect. He is the reason you're here."

"Oh, you're him." Lance said ominously.

"Shit! Heard a lot about you, my fault fool. They call me Spanish, not because I speak it, but because these niggas are racist."

"Spica please." Lance said.

"Hey! That's our word, you can't use it!" Spanish joked.

They were complete opposites as far as appearance, but the pair felt like twin personalities. Maybe they were just best friends. Lance was huge, he towered over me. Tanner had told me before that he had this guy for security and I could see why. He was a black teenager younger than me, but he was pure mass. Hopefully I'm never enemies with this guy. I heard that he was quite nice, but jeez, he was scary strong.

Spanish had full thick dark greasy hair. He was in his teens as well having peach fuzz for a mustache. However, I'm sure he was proud of his whiskers. He was dwarfed next to Lance, being possibly a full foot shorter. Spanish had a style all of his own as well. On his head was a red bandana witch matched his entire outfit. The shoes, pants, shirt and even wristband he wore was red. I wasn't sure if the color was gang related or he just had an obsession. Either way he was spunky for his size, firm athletic build.

"Never mind him, anyone cool with Tanner is cool with me. My name is Lance." He reached to shake my hand.

"Hi, Turkeys and Ostriches are both birds by the way. Just thought you should know." I said.

"Then why can't they fly?"

"Not entirely true, but whatever. Birds don't have to fly, they need to have wings."

"How you know that?"

"I know things too, what you think about a penguin, bird or not?"

"Yo you just blew my mind right now, penguins weren't even on my radar."

Tanner re-directed the conversation.

"Brian is fighting this weekend instead of Craze. He's out, we'll talk about that later."

"Welcome to the crew, you will love fight night. I run protection, but came up slinging. Knew that world way before I knew Tanner, in fact that's kind of how we met." Lance informed me.

"True and Spanish here may look young but he can hotwire anything with wheels, and some things without." Tanner chuckled.

"Shoot I can do more than that, way more. He forgot to mention all the fine honeys I Mack!"

"Not sure if I know what you just said." I smiled.

The entire room was filled with laughter.

"You are going to fit in just fine." Tanner slapped his knee.

"Quit clowning dog! You're funny now, but if I draw your number, it's real."

Spanish seemed irritated and slightly hurt that we laughed at his expense.

"Draw my number?"

"He's talking about Saturday." Tanner replied.

"What about it?"

"Everyone draws a number for their fight, matching numbers are paired up. Then the winner of each bout re-draws for the next match." Lance explained.

"How many times?"

"Depends on the number of people."

"Yeah dog and I might look small, but don't get it twisted. In that ring I'm a savage." Said Spanish.

This fight night could get out of hand. How would I be able to fight that many people? There were no weight classes, this was built to be a disaster. Lance could read the worry in my face.

"Hey, don't worry it's actually fun."

"Everyone goes down." Spanish mentioned.

"True, but it can be a game of chance." Tanner inspired.

"How so? Besides the drawing I mean."

"That's pretty much the concept of what I mean."

"Oh."

"But, every draw can have a lucky competitor. One time I was matched with a guy who fainted walking to the ring, pure luck."

The thought inspired me, who knows what I will draw on fight night. Plus if I go down early, no one will really care. It's not bare knuckle boxing, everyone has to wear gloves. Still I hadn't started training yet, which worried me.

Tanner had more pressing issues than to hear everyone bicker, he gave the drugs to Lance. My pistol was given to Spanish to get rid of as well. This was because of their individual skill sets as well as connections. He told them to sell it below street value for quick profit. To him, the golden rule of not being greedy got things done swiftly. It was all profit anyways so why think about value?

We waited for Lance and Spanish to return with the cash. He informed me that they were both orphans that he found of the street. Funny how that sounded familiar, he hid the humungous heart he had well. Spanish was orphaned by double accidental overdose. His parents were addicts looking for a new high, what they found was laced with poison. People on the street hear about a fatal O.D. and they go wild for more. There logic, is finding where the line to death is, and taking a slightly less dose.

Lance was orphaned when his mother was hit from a stray bullet in a drive-by shooting. His father was alive, but he abandoned him while still in the womb.

I knew very little about them, still I felt an understanding for them. My parents were gone for the moment, the saving grace would be if my father woke up.

Tanner had compassion for us, we were lost souls of sorrow, blending in with existence. Bonded by Brotherhood.

The small crew returned to Tanners house separately faster than I imagined. First was Lance who sold the heroin for five hundred, Tanner gave him two and sent him away. He needed Lance to continue looking for my grandfather. He said that Lance was the best chance we had at finding Slick. Spanish showed up shortly after with eight hundred for the pistol. It was surprising that the gun was worth so much on a value-deal. I wondered what true street value would be otherwise. Tanner gave Spanish three hundred dollars for his trouble. When he left, I was handed seven hundred and fifty dollars. The most money ever in my hand at once, this was a big deal.

He only kept fifty for himself. He said that it was a favor and only wanted a taste. He made a comparison on minimum wage and how he only made a few phone calls. The brunt of the work was done by his associates who were rewarded. He wanted me to feel money and understand I too could hustle and make it.

Tanner wanted me to survive in the wild. If not, then at least I had the means to return home. The amount of money in my hand could buy three tickets back. Imagine what a week of working for Tanner looked like. How much money could be earned in a month?

The cash from technical robbery was kept safe by Vince, he was like my bookkeeper. My little brother was going to plan the expenses for the trip home. He wanted to have back-up money if things went south again. Vince was big on the idea of riding out the Tanner typhoon. We were living for free while paving a way home, it just made sense to him.

The week passed in a flash after that. I trained by running and shadow boxing. There was not too much else that could be done. It was amateur boxing. We nestled in nice with Tanner. Christy took it upon herself to do laundry and clean. She was never asked to do so, but it kept her active. Vince did absolutely nothing, he slept and played games. Either way, we never over stepped our boundaries staying under another person's roof. I made Carbonara for the crew and it was a big hit, everyone enjoyed home cooked food. It was something that was lost with their parents.

My focus stayed on the fights ahead. Physically I was not prepared to fight, mentally I already won every fight. I was the champion of the night, respected by all, in my day dream. Something inside of me reached out to be known by the world. The urge for greatness.

Both of my siblings wanted to attend the event but I protested at every mention. Tanner insisted that they come in support, he insured me that they would be well protected. "Better than being at home." He said.

Ultimately they were allowed to go. Vince had to stay out of trouble, which he voiced I follow as well. Christy wanted to wear a low cut spaghetti strapped tank top. The clothing revealed too much of her blossoming youth. Last thing I needed was fighting inside and outside of the ring. She reluctantly agreed to my terms and we left for the highly anticipated fight night.

My expectations soared through the air when we were escorted in a large SUV to the fight. Tanner told me to dress normal, he brought shorts for me. I was finally going to see the anticipated wonder.

In Kansas City, Missouri there are thousands of possible venues for such use. Where would he take us? The car drove down towards the river. There was a casino actually floating on the river.

For a moment I believed that the affair was somehow inside the casino. We slowed as we neared the casino and parked in the parking lot. Confused, Tanner informed me that "We're going to do a little walking."

Our driver stayed in the vehicle with a radio. He was the lookout guy. Tanner led us to a fence near the parking lot, there was a section with a secret entrance cut back. He folded the fence back leading us close to the river. Apparently the Casino used to be much smaller and operated on strict regulation. It dodged sanctions by building on top of giant river floats. Our event was held at the old abandoned casino and it was marvelous.

Walking to the building there was no noise, it seemed vacant. Perhaps we were to set up the match. The old casino doors were conveniently unlocked and we continued inside the building. Tanner led us down the hallway and I began to hear the roar of a crowd. The noise grew with proximity, fueling my anxiety for the night.

The spectacle was amazing. Every detail of the room resembled a professional match. The casino was legit and surprisingly clean. Our ring looked like an actual boxing ring, with a man ready to referee inside. There were ring girls in bikinis for the match counts. Tanner had a refreshment stand set up as well.

"Now you see the magic."

He instructed Vince and Christy to their seats while we went to get ready. We passed Lance close to the ring. There was no fight drawn yet, but people could take action on the names. We were like baseball cards to these guys. They wanted to know how much I weighed, my height, age & last time I had sex. We got pretty personal.

I was led to a room with all the fighters, who were practicing with the space provided. Spanish was among the fighters. The numbers worked out that there were fifteen fighters. This meant that Tanner would act as a wild card for the second round of drawing, so it also had even fights. With fourteen fighters there would be seven winners from the first draw. The odd number winner would just fight Tanner essentially. It was undoubtedly an advantage, which he argued worked for reasons of ownership.

The third round of draws would only have four fighters remaining. Then two for the final fight.

Each fight lasted three rounds, three minutes a piece. This meant that if I fought every round of the tournament it would total forty five minutes. My mental edge began to fail at the thought of the true odds. I argued in my head about fight outcomes, what if one fight lasted one round?

Tanner informed me that between each fight was at least ten minutes. The gauntlet felt possible, there was fifteen hundred dollars in the winner's pot. To me that meant more than respect, I wanted cash.

We were all given a piece of paper to sign our names, fold the paper and drop it into a hat. Of course no one followed the instructions. Most names were misspelled or hard to read. The fighters ranged from a wide group of people. From five foot five to six foot three. There were no weight divisions, this was just hood. A few of the guys looked like boxers, typical. I'm not sure why I thought that it would be easy to win any fight. This was going to be a challenge, finally we drew names.

The pairs were as follows:

Jim S. vs. Spanish

Ruthless vs. Ox

Cody vs. Mike

Lo vs. Dre.

Bone vs. Kent

Drew vs. Victor

La La vs. Mike H.

The guy that I was matched with appeared to be the easiest. His name was written as *Ruthless*, but he was clearly out of shape. He was over confident if anything. The fights started and as a spectator the tournament, it was fun, being a competitor was a blast.

Spanish went down in the first round thirty seconds into the match. He says that it was a cheap shot, but who knows.

My fight went according to planned. It was a bit scary fighting for sport instead of survival. Things were different, I was hesitant to even hit the guy. When he landed a haymaker things changed, it awakened my rage. I felt his full power behind that hit, the blow rocked me but he was exhausted. The bell rang for the first round and I was ready for more, he was not however. After a slurry of combos he fell to the mat, he reached for the ropes. My opponent was only able to pull himself halfway during the countdown. Christy jumped for joy when it was announced that I won by knock out. Tanner rushed in the ring and hugged me to congratulate my win. He reminded me there was a chance we would fight, now that I made it to the next drawing.

This was not something I wanted, my fear and affection for Tanner wouldn't allow me to fight him. The fights went on for around forty minutes after my fight. I was fully refreshed and limber, the edge was in my favor. The high from fighting sky-rocketed my adrenaline.

Other fights were pretty even and few were unpredictable. Victor was a Mexican guy covered in tattoos. My first perception of him, was him being pushed around easily. I was wrong. He dominated his first fight with wicked precision. Victor was fast beyond belief and was my only worry other than fighting Tanner.

Dre was the tallest guy fighting, his fight stood out as well but for a different reason. The bell rang to end the first round of his fight. His opponent "*Lo*" Struck him after the signal. Dre became angry at the cheap shot and knocked him out at the start of the next round. Lo was out cold, he should have respected the bell.

This left three of the eight names unwanted for matches. I did not want to draw Dre, Tanner or Victor. That would be ultimate Strength, training and speed.

The time came that we draw again and it was announced as follows:

Jim S. vs. Ox

Victor vs. Cody

Dre vs. Kent

Mike H. vs. Tanner

Again luck had given me a better card. This Jim guy was an out of towner and a boxer, he was well trained. This would be the end of the line for me, except I outweighed him by forty pounds at least. He was fast, but it felt like being hit by my sister. Suppose that is where the term originated. Had he knocked out in the first round with only ten seconds to spare.

Tanner won his fight by decision, it went all three rounds in his favor. He never got aggressive, just sparred around a bit. Maybe he was reserving his energy for a harder match.

Dre won Kent by knockout first round and Victor scored a staggering decision victory over Cody. They were about the same size, but he remained untouched the entire fight. Cody was a friend of Tanner's, he fought every fight night.

The third round of draws were brutal and exhausting.

Tanner vs. Victor

These bouts were ugly, Tanner went toe to toe with Victor. Every hit exchanged excited the crowd. Skill vs speed were so thrilling to watch. The winner was chosen after a blistering three rounds of punishment to one another. Victor became the Victor, pun intended. Tanner loved the match, he exchanged information with Victor post fight. To him this was the most fun he ever had. After fighting by his side and for Tanner, I felt the same way.

My fight with Dre was worrisome from my first blow. He felt nothing, I felt fighting Jim. Every time Dre landed a jab my ears began to ring, before my vision blurred. This man was strong and knew how to hit with gloves on. With rules this man was unstoppable, this fight wasn't the streets. Even though it was an illegal gambling ring underground. I couldn't kick him.

When the first round ended my energy was gone. The guy was simply too big to fight with gloves on. Before the end of the second round he earned the K.O. I fell hard and didn't try hard to get back up.

Though both Tanner and I had lost, we were happy regardless. We watched the final fight between Dre and Victor as excited spectators.

Oh what a sight it was, somehow speed had the upper hand. After three rounds Dre was exhausted chasing his opponent around the ring. He grew tired of getting constantly hit. Victor would punch and run to wear out Dre, who was much larger. The third round was a brutal tear down of Dre, he just did not have enough energy to block a single punch. His arms fell and soon, so did his jaw. Victor took home the prize money that night, it was well deserved.

By the end of the night Tanner told me it was time to leave, I collected my siblings. My brother needed to cash out first before going to the car. Apparently he had been betting all night.

That was where the true money came from. Not from fighting, but from gambling on every fight, round and fighter. Vince had bet on me till I lost, he then double downed and put all his money on Victor. Vince returned with me to the car carrying one thousand dollars. He started the night with two hundred that Vince says he borrowed from me. Some safe he turned out to be. Though I can't judge too harsh, he did grow the fund. Even after losing a bet.

We left with money smiles and stories. Who does this stuff? And who in their right mind would take his family? This is not something I'll ever regret. It was my first of many fight nights.

When we arrived back at Tanners house he had beer ready and waiting. We celebrated, he invited over some girls and a few friends. Christy went to bed early, thank God!

Vince actually partied with us that night. He had beer which I hoped was his first, but he enjoyed it too much.

Vince liked to go to parties in high school, why should tonight be any different. He had a breakdown of each of my fights, to Vince I just became a celebrity. This was a big deal.

Tanner had some brushes on his face showing signs of a scuffle. I on the other hand had a huge knot on my head. My eye was blood shot on one side, definitely from fighting Dre. Tanner said it would go away in a few days.

The night turned to early morning it was nearly three before Spanish showed up with Lance. They brought more girls and the party elevated with louder music and rooms full of smoke. I turned down the chance to smoke weed several times. I wanted to stay sober-ish. A beautiful Latina girl approached me and asked if I wanted a shotgun. Immediately the answer yes spewed out of my mouth, not knowing what it was. I assumed that it was a drink of some sort, or an alcoholic shot.

She took a cigar from the cleavage in her shirt to light it up. It was nerve racking, the last thing I needed was a drug habit. The alcohol in my system was already making me impaired.

She told me to "Relax" as she puffed the blunt away. Then she knocked away the ash from the ember of the cigar. She turned the blunt around, putting the lit end in her mouth. Her arms wrapped around my neck, I opened my mouth. She sent second hand smoke out from the mouthpiece of the cigar. My hands slid to her hips and began to move lower. I started coughing sporadically. The smoke burned in my chest, smoke was trying to escape my lungs, I started gasping for air. The girl was very sweet and rubbed my back as I coughed up a lung. She knew this was my first time. When my coughing had ceased my eyes watered. It was as if the world became clearer in my mind. Everything looked altered like I wouldn't have noticed before. The wall paper stood out from the room and certain sounds were easier to pick up on.

"My name is Trisha." The girl whispered in my ear.

"Brian." I smiled.

She made the first move, maybe she was a she-wolf. Trisha wasted no time for small talk. Within a few minutes of talking I was already reaching second base. My little sister was already asleep in the bedroom, but I still had an unused room in the basement. Trisha and I took the passion downstairs to the extra room. The rest of the night was dark for me, I blacked out. Her body was very memorable though. When she started to unclothe I thought that she was too much for me to handle. Trisha was voluptuous with tattoos near sensitive areas. From what I remember she was amazing and even provided protection.

The next morning I heard a man screaming Trisha's name from outside the house. Tanner was awake and ready to check the commotion. He proceeded with his 9mm to the front door. He already knew who was there yelling, but I did not pick up as quick.

When I looked out the window Tanner was standing in front of Trisha holding his gun. The guy yelling was eight ball, suddenly I put two and two together. She must have been his girl, Tanner mentioned this before. Meaning she cheated twice and it looked like with Tanner both times. This was bad it was me who was responsible, or was it her?

I was caught peering through the window just as eight ball accused them of sleeping together. He saw my face and recognized me from the fight. He had been looking for me ever since that day, leaving Tanner alone for the insult. Eight ball didn't believe that Trisha stayed the night at Tanners with nothing happening. But his rage was amplified by the thought of me and Trisha.

"You!" Eight ball pointed at my face through the window.

Trisha and Tanner looked back to see an empty window. I had already disappeared from the drama, peering through another window.

"You've been hiding him? Who is he?"

"I don't know what you're talking about."

"He's dead, you're dead. You are both fucking dead." Eight ball left furious with Trisha rushing behind him. She was relentless to catch up.

With that Tanner retreated to the house. My demeanor was tilted towards embarrassment.

"Was that his girl?"

"Yeah." He nodded.

"Shit how come no one told me?"

"Vince saw you with her, but he doesn't know who she is."

"What happened after I laid down?"

"Well your brother is hilarious first off, we pretty much just stayed up all night laughing."

"While I slept with the neighborhood Frisbee."

Tanner looked confused.

"Because she gets passed around so much." I said.

"Oh, no one plays that game here. It would be funnier if you said football."

"Should have said football Brian." Vince muttered from the couch half conscious.

Tanner laughed continuously.

"See? The kids freaking wild man."

I was unamused, to me another enemy was added to my list. He was already on that list, but is now a higher threat. This guy probably wanted me dead for real. I beat him up after a low blow and regretfully slept with his girlfriend. Tanner assured me that nothing would happen as long as he had my back. It comforted me to know I was protected and valuable.

The day after the fight we started looking for new locations. Tanner took me with him for every possible lead this time. He wanted me to learn his methods so I could apply them anywhere. Tanner told me that I had earned his trust in a very short amount of time, the least he could do is take me to school.

He would pay people a reward for finding discrete buildings, if it was used then he threw in extra money as a bonus. I asked why we didn't use the same location twice. He recapitulated his desire to remain out of jail.

"It's all about playing the game kid, one wrong move & they throw away the key." He said.

We searched every day for the perfect spot to have the next fight night. My job was mostly sitting and talking for hours in a vehicle. Each day we received updates on the search for my family, they were mostly just second hand encounters. The word was out that Ox was looking for Slick, so anytime someone brought information forward it was usually useless. One story was that he went back to Mexico after a massacre. Another said that he died a few years back, each piece of information had a common trait. Slick was gone without notice, no one fully knew where he was or if he was even alive still.

We drank beer, played pool and watched television in our free time. The days melted together from repetition and soon I found that week's turned into months almost. Within that timeframe little else happened. All investigations leading to my grandpa were failed. The fight nights went just as planned every two weeks. I participated in every fight night, but never won. It justly felt like a game of chance to win. Tanner took Christy and Vince to the Zoo to get away from the city a few times. They loved the trips, but to me it was still in the city. Christy got better at baking and started working on biscuits every morning. In the afternoons she made different kinds of breads and rolls. Tanner kept the kitchen well stocked for her experimentation.

I had Lance call the hospital inquiring about my father each week. He was still unresponsive, so we never left back home. It was hard to tell my siblings each week that our father was in the same condition. We were happy with Tanner, but still felt lost without Eli.

The days were still filled with joy at the fellowship from one another. We had no school, no real job, and it was a time where everyone just did what they wanted. It was liberating to be so free through this period. By this time, we had close to five thousand dollars saved.

Tanner seemed to love us like we were his missing family. The conversations we would have on each stake-out were ridiculous. We talked about super hero match ups, who would win? Girls, cars, sports, and Japanese trading card games. He was the older brother I never had, but always wanted.

Lance would come over to hang out with Vince, when he wasn't on duty for Tanner. Everyone treasured my little brother. He was cynical and well beyond his years. Spanish would try to linger and talk to Christy, but I constantly interceded and kicked him out. She was attracting the wrong guys through puberty and I was having none of it. That was another good thing about becoming a fighter. I was never afraid to whoop some ass, if need be.

Eight ball tried to crash one of the fight nights, but he wouldn't dare cross the security. He would basically have to slaughter the entire room or be killed if he crossed the line at the events. There were always "Big" names there with their own security as well. Even still he let me know that I was on his radar and not leaving anytime soon.

The earnings from each week of working and from gambling on fight night, were set aside by Vince. I stopped caring about how much we had. Everything seemed pointless if dad was broken and grandpa lost. By this time my Grandpa Christy would be back from Ireland, we could live with him, but I was having too much fun. He was old school, living with him would be extremely strict and I would probably be working two jobs at eighteen. It dawned on me the moment I thought about time, I realized it was almost my birthday already. My graduation would be missed regrettably, but school was the last thing on my mind.

There was something different about me on my eighteenth birthday. I had a family again and was finding my own way. Tanner ended up throwing me a party to celebrate me being legal. I was becoming well known around the area by then and it was overwhelming.

For Tanner, throwing a huge party was an honor. He filled the house with people from all over the state. Insisting on a two to one ratio for girls to guys. He invited every pretty girl he saw and some ugly ones as well.

Tanner would say "We all need a girl in our price range."

This idea was genius, but kind of mean when I thought about it. Vince was on board for the party and followed Tanner like a shadow. He wanted to increase his value by being associated with the host. To be fair, Vince was not far from adulthood he would turn seventeen not long after my birthday. He was just over a year younger than I was, so it was right that he be treated as such.

Christy approached me before the party started. She had a wrapped gift in her hands, I also noticed that she straightened her hair. This frightened me because she probably wanted to be at the party.

"Happy birthday Brian! Vince and I got you something." She kissed me on the cheek.

"You didn't have to get me anything sis, oh and your hair looks nice."

"Thanks, I straightened it."

My siblings had wrapped a box inside of a box, which caused me to believe that it would go on forever. But I was wrong, inside the second container was a golden pendent with the letters "OX" it would fit perfect on the necklace dad gave me.

"Do you like it?"

"I love it! Thank you so much. How did you even find something like this?" I hugged my sister.

"Tanner took us to the mall instead of the zoo, it was a secret for your birthday so you couldn't be there."

"That's why you guys went to the zoo so much?"

"Well we went twice, because you can't appreciate all the animals in one day. But three times, c'mon Brian. That was a dead giveaway."

"You're the devil"

"Shut up Brian, anyways I'll be in my room all night so you can enjoy yourself."

"Wait, you didn't get dressed up because of the party?"

"Oh Brian, girls just want to feel pretty some days. You should learn that."

Christy returned to the basement with a bowl full of cookie dough and a glass of milk. She planned on eating every last bite of that dough. I knew she was growing up, but our situation propelled her youth. My sister was learning about the world and how it changed. I never thought that she would change with it.

Welcome to the Family

Everywhere I turned was a body, the house could not possibly fit another person, so people started congregating in the back yard and front of Tanners house. People wanted to take shots with me or bong rips, on the account of my birthday. I declined until the offer flipped to shotguns and body shots. The basement was locked, Christy was in her own world and Vince wandered around the house meeting people. The party seemed less stressful, I was talking to everyone like we knew each other for years. I wanted to let loose and become the life of the party, I was a social whore that night. On my birthday I should have the right to get a little crazy. There were so few guys at the party, most of the ones there were outside listening to one loud guy's story. He was drunk as hell, but he was stealing the spotlight. People were laughing at his every word, though it might have been from his accent. He had a thick New York/Brooklyn sort of sound to his voice, it was abrasive but accepted. They loved how brash he was, I had to listen in for myself.

"So I've been sleeping with this chick right, and every time I stay at her house, her fag of a brother tries to fuck me."

People laugh thinking they heard the punch line.

"No seriously, I can't make this shit up. Every time we stay there he comes on to me. Pinching my ass, rubbing against me, blowing me kisses."

The group surrounding the drunk man grows in size. He gets even louder.

"So I get pissed one day and go off on him, saying 'Preston your sister can do stuff you can't do! Leave me alone! You got nothing to offer!' So the next night I wake up to a blow job that's freaking fantastic. So I peak under the covers and see Preston. So I yelled 'What are you doing?!'"

"What did he say?" Asks a guy listening to his story.

"Something my sister can't do."

Everyone in the group laughed, it had a turn at the end of the joke that he sold well. I thought the guy was a violent homophobic, but he twisted the ending to poke fun at himself. It was easy to see why he had a crowd, the guy was like a stand-up comedian. He had so many funny stories, one after another. One of his rants started with "The second time I ever stole a cop car." The first line alone made me laugh out loud. Everything was perfect, but for some strange reason I felt alone at the party. It could have been from drinking, but I kept thinking of Angel.

I sat on a stoop in the corner of the house away from people, trying to wallow in my own misery. Somehow Tanner found coming out of the house with two beers, he tossed me one.

"What's wrong kid? You look like your freaking cat died."

"Just thinking bro."

"You didn't like the comedian that came?" Tanner pointed to the man telling stories in the yard.

"That explains a lot, yeah that guy is funny as hell."

"Then what's up kid? You should be enjoying yourself."

I paused for a moment. "My dad is still in a comma and I still think about Angel."

"Is that the girl you said dropped you?"

"Yeah, but⋯"

"She's not worth it Brian, girls come & go." He sipped his beer.

"Easier said than done. It's hard to let go because of how I felt for her, not how she felt towards me."

"Brian, I get that bro better than anyone, you don't think Tanner Brady has never been in love?"

"I never said that."

"Exactly, focus on the here and now Brian. Forget the past, it's already gone."

"Yeah but in the here and now I think about my dad never waking up. What do I do then?"

Tanner messed up my hair with his hand and took a sip of his beer. He was showing affection & making light of the pain that was a reality.

"You know, someone wise once told me that 'we are only burdened with what we can handle.'" Tanner said in a firm voice.

"What happens when we can't take the burden anymore?"

"We die, you're not dead are you?" Tanner smiled.

"No."

I finally drank some of the beer he brought.

"Well then you must be able to handle this one. You're one of the strongest people I've ever met Brian. A lot of people have so much given to them, some have never worked a day in their lives. Do you know what they are?"

"Spoiled?" I guessed.

"Weak, they couldn't handle one day in the real world, and that is exactly why they were given everything. If they had to feed themselves, they would starve."

"I suppose you're right."

"Damn straight I am. Now are you ready to have some fun?" Tanner said.

"Yeah, thanks man." I hugged Tanner.

"Don't mention it brother, just next time you tell the story let me be the wise man and you give the advice."

"That's deep man."

"What can I say? Oh there is a birthday present waiting for you out front. Why don't you go check it out?"

He threw a set of keys to me. They were car keys for sure.

"What's this?"

"Keys dummy."

"Keys to what?"

"That old beater sitting out front."

There was an old rusty truck out front of the house. It was at least thirty years old covered in dirt.

"You are giving me that truck?"

"You deserve it, she's not much, but it will make it to see your father."

"You mean it? What about Christy and Vince?"

"They can go or stay, up to you guys. Go see your dad, and find that girl you think about."

"Thank you so much, this means the world to me."

"Okay, enough mushy crap. Enjoy the party tonight and plan your trip tomorrow."

"It's already a night to remember."

"Shoot, there are six strippers here and they are all in the living room with Vince."

"Seriously? Like stripping?"

"No, but who knows by now. We've been out here for a while." Tanner joked.

"Guess I better get inside."

The house was filled with smoke, most who remained inside didn't notice. I came from the outside so the rooms tasted like different ash trays. Spanish was stoned playing video games with Lance. Everyone else sort of thinned out, like the wild party was outside and a chill version inside. There were a bunch of people that just fell asleep. Vince was one of them, he was passed out on two strippers who all napped on the couch. It was either cute or creepy, still haven't decided what I think about that picture. Christy was still in her room, it was only right that I check on her as well. She was watching cartoons half-awake next to an empty bowl that used to house cookie dough. Her glass of milk was still mostly full, which concerned me for the level of raw eggs she probably consumed.

"Hey Brian, how is your birthday going?"

"Good, but I'm kind of tired. It's been a long day."

"Is everything okay?" Christy asked concerned.

"It's more than okay, look." I showed Christy the keys to the truck outside.

"What's that for?"

"Keys to a truck that Tanner gave me for my birthday."

"Oh my God Brian! He bought you a truck?" Christy said surprised.

"Well, yeah, but it's not like a brand new truck. The thing is a dinosaur and knowing Tanner, he got it on an insane deal or bet."

"Maybe so, but he didn't have to get you anything Brian." Christy pointed out.

"Yeah, I'm grateful sis, I really am."

"Just making sure Brian, does this mean that we are going home?"

"Yep, maybe day after tomorrow if you want to. Tanner said you or Vince could stay too, it up to you."

"So we are coming back?"

"More than likely, unless dad wakes up the moment we get there."

"I don't want to see him Brian."

"Why not?"

"Because it's hard enough to always think about him, I just can't see him like that right now."

"I understand, you don't have to come."

"Hold you horses, I do want to go, just not to see dad. There is stuff at the house that I want."

"Fair enough, tomorrow I'll tell Vince, goodnight sis. Love you."

"Love you too Brian, happy birthday!"

The next morning I woke up early while most were hung over. Tanner was already awake waiting on me. He sat drinking coffee in the kitchen, wearing his tank top and chain.

"So, how'd it go Brian? Did you have a good birthday?" He asked me.

"How are you always awake?"

"Coffee my man, it's a terrible drug."

"That makes sense I guess. Thank you for everything, it could not have been a better eighteenth."

"You fell asleep before the magician showed up, so it could technically be better." Tanner bragged.

"There was a magician? That would have been so cool! I love magic, ugh, stupid sleep."

"Nah, I'm just messing with you kid."

"Oh thank God, I was starting to get bummed out."

"Maybe we can see a magic show if you guys come back."

"Do you think we won't come back?"

"I never think anything, we are all here by choice. It would be ideal that you find what you're looking for and never come back. Go become a doctor or something, you don't need to fight to survive. Just use that head of yours." Tanner poured another glass of coffee.

"What if we do come back?" I asked, concerned he was kicking us out.

"If that happens, then you better bring me back a souvenir from bum fuck Egypt or whatever Kansas town you come from." Tanner said while trying to light a cigarette.

I knew that he wanted the best for us, we were like guests in his house before becoming a family.

"I'll bring you back some corn, that's closer to what we have."

"Oh, spare me! Sheesh, I just could not live outside the city." Tanner said judging me.

"It's a suburban area, but it's still a city." I shrugged.

"Do you have gangs?"

"Good point. Never mind." I laughed at his comparison.

"When are you guys heading out?"

"Anytime now, Vince and Christy are getting ready."

Tanner stood up and tucked the front of his shirt behind his belt buckle.

"Well, tell the kids goodbye for me. There is some business I have to address. Be safe Brian."

He gave me a hug (not like him) and went on his way. I think that he just wasn't good at saying goodbye. Tanner had already accepted that we might find something better. We had money to do so, because of him. He was just giving us the second chance we needed, he didn't expect to become attached. Tanner left just as my siblings came upstairs. We ate breakfast and packed sandwiches for the trip. My brother was sleepwalking until we left. I could tell because he did not touch his food at all. It was nearly nine in the morning, but Vince probably woke up after I went to sleep. I imagine he partied pretty hard last night, nothing ever gets in the way of Vince a food, nothing!

Vince slept the entire trip until Wichita. It took about three and a half hours to get there. Though we stopped multiple times for candy and snacks. My brother was supposed to navigate the trip but he failed me. The truck we were in was spacious for a single cab pick-up, so it made for a nice bed. We made it back home in Derby, Kansas. After months of being missing, we knew the heat was low, but relevant. Still I didn't know the state of the house. Someone could have issued a warrant at some point and checked to see if we were hiding in the house. So the front and back door were probably locked, or closed off.

All of the windows were locked as well. This was a minor setback unbeknownst to police, we had Vince with us. He got into the house through the attic and let us in through his bedroom window.

Coming inside it was clear that an intruders had been there. Things were ransacked and thrown everywhere, but there was a kind soul in the bunch. One officer must have thrown away everything that would spoil in the fridge. We only had soda and water there after breaking into our old home.

Christy went straight for her room, she missed her own space. Vince and I went to the kitchen, neither of us were hungry. Instead we were rather curious as to what food there was in the house.

Vince found canned Ravioli in the pantry & random vegetables. There wasn't much at all, almost like the cops slept in our beds and ate our food. If not them, then definitely squatters.

Vince started making himself a belated breakfast, he slept through all of our snack breaks too.

"I'm going to take off soon, you think you'll be fine here while I'm gone?"

"Brian, we were homeless before. I think we will be okay." Vince replied.

"Okay, well I'm going to run and tell your sister real quick and then I'll leave. Maybe I should come through your window again just to be safe."

"Yeah that sounds good, by the time you get back Christy and I will be passed out anyways."

My worrisome nature had passed, there was a lot less danger of trouble in Derby. Tanner had endless locks on his doors and bars for each window. In Kansas there was little need for such things. We lived in a nicer suburb so I was clear minded. Christy looked passed out when I went to go check on her. The bed was just one giant pile of frizz, she must have been exhausted from her late night movie marathon. I didn't want to wake her so I tip-toed into her room and gave her a kiss on atop of her head. As I walked away, there was a faint whisper.

"Bye, love you, be safe." Christy muttered.

I turned back and softly replied. "Love you too, I will."

My siblings laid low while in my absence to see my father. They could be in their bedrooms; but if any outside noise came, then immediately they must flee to the attic. When I returned we would meet in the attic, this was discussed during the trip. I made Vince repeat it back to me just to be sure. The hospital was only about a ten or fifteen minute drive, way easier than taking the bus.

Lance had already found out what floor Eli was on. He was taken to a special ward on the second level with his own room.

I was on pins and needles passing each room. Looking inside from a far all I could see was suffering in every room.

"Who are you looking for?" A nurse asked.

"Eli Vega."

"Are you a relative?" She quivered.

"Cousin, second cousin."

"Hmm, what's your name?"

"Benjamin Flacked" I said with haste hoping to sell her.

"Hmm, he's in room two thirty-seven, on the other side down the hall."

The nurse walked away with no further questions. She snickered as if she proved to have thoroughly investigated my background. Paranoia served me well in quick thinking. For some reason I already had a past for this false alias, as if I were a spy.

"Benjamin Flacked, a student from Ohio state taking the year off to soul search."

It sounded believable to me.

My mind ran wild when I saw my father. He had improved, his face was healed. Also he had full-on beard. I almost didn't recognize him at first. Dad just laid still, breathing slowly. He might have been lost forever, or maybe he could hear my voice.

"Dad?" I checked for consciousness "Can you hear me? It's me Brian. Don't worry dad we're okay. Me and the kids I mean. We miss you, please just come back. We need you dad, please? I need you···"

Floodgates opened, my sobbing was necessary. This was the time to let loose and lay on his frame hoping for relief. He showed no sign of awareness, an empty body. There was a time when he was a superhero to me, now all my heroes have fallen. Resentment ensued for the ones who inflicted this pain of my family.

"Dad not sure if you can hear me, but whoever did this to you is going to pay. That's a promise."

I left the hospital feeling helpless, my life was in shambles. Some part of me thought that my father would come through. But, seeing him again with my own eyes changes things. There is nothing to do to help my father. All I could do was watch after my siblings in his absence. Months had already passed and we were doing just fine in the real world alone. My father was not able to see my successes in failure. It hurt my heart to know this was it, I was alone.

Vince and Christy were waiting for me back at the house, but before then I had some unfinished business. I wanted to see Angel before leaving. She might change her mind and come with us, she was always on my mind. It was my fault for not trying hard enough. She deserved better and this time there would be nothing that stopped me. Angel was mine, simple as that.

I drove past her old house, but it was empty. Maybe they were evicted, either way I'd find her. I still didn't have a phone, or her number for that matter. Instead I decided to follow up on another lead. Her best friend Courtney worked at a local coffee house. She was my age, we had Biology together in school. I found out freshman year, she had a crush on me, after getting with Angel. It was awkward at the time, but her affection never left. She was always nice to me, it was easy to see she still liked me. So I decided to exploit that information to find Angel

The coffee shop was near to where I was anyways. From the outside I could see Courtney through the window working. She looked exactly the same, just older. She was actually very cute, her long blonde hair suited her personality, and she talked like a princess. I sat in her section, waiting for her to notice me.

"Hello, what can I get for you today darling?"

"Hi, Courtney"

"Brian? Oh my God! No one has seen you since high school, you look good. How have you been?"

She grabbed my arm and reached in for a hug.

"I've been doing well, just got into town actually."

"Oh right, there were a lot of rumors after you left, we heard you joined the army."

I snickered. "No, nothing like that. I just did a bit of traveling."

"That's awesome! I want to travel too someday, just waiting for Mr. Right." She said nervously.

"You'll find him, you're a cute girl."

"Really?"

"Hell yeah, don't settle for less either."

"Wow, thanks Brian." She said brushing her hair.

"Anytime beautiful, hey by the way, do you still talk to Angel?"

"Oh yeah, we are still friends. So how long you in town for?"

"Not very long, where can I find her?"

She was dodging my question, trying to redirect the conversation.

"Well, I don't know, she has changed Brian."

"I understand, so does she live around here? Her house was vacant."

"Oh they were kicked out, she lives somewhere else now."

"And where would that be?" I asked passively.

Courtney looked disappointed, she did not want to talk about Angel.

"Did you only come here to ask about her?"

"What? Of course not!"

She crossed her arms. "Really Brian?"

"Hey, I'm serious now. It took a lot to even come in here."

"Yeah, why is that?" She pouted.

"Because Courtney I've had feelings for you a long time now. I just wanted to wait before asking you out too soon."

She smiled with glee.

"Brian, I don't know what to say. We have known each other so long. Is this a real thing?"

"Yes, but it had to be right. That's why I wanted to see Angel. I needed to ask her permission to date you."

"You don't need her approval Brian. That bitch doesn't run me."
Her mood shifted.

"I know, but it has to be right. Is there any way we could talk to
her, she needs to know about us."

To my astonishment Courtney believed every word I said and
thought me sweet for thinking of Angel's feelings.

"There is a party tonight, she will be there."

"Perfect, I could meet you there then."

"Brian, Angel really did change. She's not even the same
anymore."

I attempted to distract Courtney.

"Hey, have your eyes always been that blue?"

"Well they change colors sometimes⋯" She said flustered.

"They are beautiful, just stunning. Look, we can ditch the party if
it's lame, let just poke our heads in. What do you say?"

"Okay, yeah why not. I mean it will probably be totally lame
anyways. Here let me write down the address."

"Bet, what time you get off?"

"Three, but the party is at eight."

"Sounds good how bout' I meet you around nine then?"

"That sounds good."

"It's a date then, you should wear something that matches your eyes."

"Oh for sure, think I have something cute, can't wait." Her face filled with joy.

"Me either."

I left a twenty dollar bill on the table for coffee and tip, and walked out with the address. Upon getting back to the house I realized that I never ordered anything. Not even coffee, I just left a tip for nothing, hopefully she didn't think ill intentions.

I climbed through Vince's window and to my surprise, he was wide awake. He brought his video games with him and played them while I was gone.

"Hey Brian, how did it go? Did you see dad?"

"Yeah."

"How was he?"

"Not good bud, it was hard to see him like that again."

"Don't tell me, I don't want to know." He said with a controller in his hands.

"That's fair."

"Are you ready to go now? This game is not as fun as I remember."

"Oh, there is still one more thing to do."

"Like what?"

"Well Angel might come with us."

"What! Brian, there is no way in hell she will fit in that truck!"

It was funny that space was his only concern.

"Yeah I get it, but KC is only a few hours away, we'd get by if needed."

"Great, just awesome, the more the merrier."

"Where is Christy?"

"How the hell should I know?"

"Ugh! C'mon Vince!"

I stormed out of his room to check on my sister. Thankfully she was still sound asleep in her bed.

She awoke confused and shaken. I prompted her to sleep and that we would leave in the morning. Funny how my sister was treated compared to the Vince.

I rested that afternoon and showered before the party. My thoughts surrounded Angel, I had missed her. It was time to show her how much I have changed.

The party was going pretty hard by the time I arrived, it was easy to find. I got there just before nine, trying to get there early. My hope was that I could find Angel before Courtney showed up. The entrance to the house was wide open and people were drinking out front. Courtney should have told me whose party it was. I had no clue what I was walking into, just the will of fire burning through my veins. The best way to find someone is normally by asking, so I asked random people about Angel.

"Hey bro you know where Angel is?"

"Who?" A guy responded.

"No one, never mind." First guy was a bust, drunk girl next.

"Have you seen Angel?"

"Hey you're kind of cute, what's your name?"

Never mind, drunk girl was a mistake. I quickly walked away ignoring her and on to the next.

"You know where I can find Angel?"

"Nah man sorry." A man said.

I moved up and down the party trying to recognize someone. There was a chance that she was not there yet. So I sat in the corner and wanted for a sign. While I was seated there was a girl who passed by me multiple times. To and from the kitchen or living room of the house. She must have known the place well, there was my sign.

"Hey, you don't happen to know Angel do you babe?"

"Yeah man, that's my bitch!"

"Have you seen her? I'm her cousin Dan." Again with a quick alias.

"Oh right on, yeah man she is upstairs in her room. It's the door on the right."

"Thanks babe."

Now I knew that she lived here, it must have been her part. Filled with excitement I leapt up the stairs to her room. It's not like me to knock before entering and this time was a mistake. I opened her door to find her half-naked. She was undressing in front of another guy who sat on the bed. The guy noticed me first and freaked out.

"Whoa! Buzz off man! Can't you see we're busy?"

I ignored his words when my eyes met with Angels. Then I saw red, there was nothing else. I tackled the man to the ground, he struggled to get up. That is when my knee flew into his face throwing him sideways. I grabbed his long shaggy hair to pull him towards the bed. He swung wide and foolishly, I retorted with a head-butt that knocked him unconscious with a broken nose.

"Brian?" Angel said. "What are you doing? I mean you're alive?"

I left the room without a response. She was just another girl to me now. Her boyfriend would gain back consciousness soon anyways.

"Brian don't leave,   please?" She yelled from the top of the stairs.

Part of me wanted to hear what she had to say. I briefly paused losing valuable time on my casual escape. I turned to look Angel in the eyes one last time.

"There's just never a good time for 'us' is there?"

Those were the words that I left her with, walking to the door. By the time I reached the front door a voice yelled from atop the stairs. It was Angel's boyfriend.

"Get that guy! He just robbed me!" He lied.

What a way to start a riot, the entire party seemed to stop and look at me. I knew things were about to get rough.

"Fine. Let's see what happens." I said casually.

The moment I finished my sentence someone rushed me in a plaid button-up. He was received by a kick to the groin and a slug in the mouth. The groin shot was for his shitty shirt.

Two more gents hurried in to be heroes. One was on the larger side and looked like he could take a hit. The other guy was average looking, but to me, he looked fragile. The smaller one clearly had no business being involved. I throat punched the big guy and gave the little guy a quick pop in the mouth. Fight night had paid off tremendously, I wasn't scared in the least bit. Instead I was having fun.

"Yeah! Who's next?"

I was answered with a guy jumping on my back, trying to choke me out. He distracted me while another man landed some cheap shots. They thought they had me, I resisted and almost broke free. Then a girl and her boyfriend tried to hold back one of my arms. I was immobilized for a moment, then focused. You cannot trap an Alpha Wolf alive, the fight was far from over. The guy behind me let-go of my neck when I broke his teeth with the back of my skull. I thrusted my head like a reverse head-butt. My rage wouldn't allow failure. Eli said to never hit a lady, but I shoved the shit out of the one who had my arm. Her boyfriend got elbowed in the chest before being socked in the jaw.

Why not finish off the party with a bang. One of the guys I knocked out had friends and family there. I was attacked by people who wanted me dead, it was obvious. They started to throw glass bottles and use weapons that would take me out instantly, if I were caught. My survival skills kicked in high gear. Almost as if I became a Kung Fu genius, there was no stopping my war rampage. I was not going to die because I had things to do, these people were in my way. A guy hit me on my back with a club or something, so I kicked him in the chest. He flew towards the wall and my elbow followed to end him. Someone threw a bottle at my face and I caught it, mid-air. My hands threw the empty bottle back at the aggressor, like a grenade. It shattered in his face, scaring him for life.

Tables became weapons, lamps were weapons, everything was game to use. Before I knew it the entire party was laid out cold. Some with concussions or broken limbs, there would be a line at the E.R. that night. Those who backed down or fled, had one hell of a story. There was only one person left that wanted a piece of Mr. Brian Vega.   Angel's new boyfriend that I already beat-up. Why won't he learn? Can't he just look around him and see the carnage?

He persisted carrying a baseball bat ready to do some damage. I underestimated his swing, it landed dead center of my ribs. The blow broke two ribs, but it also sent a surge of adrenaline down my spine. I jerked the bat out of his hand and tuned the weapon against him, slamming him to the ground and kicking his ribs. I broke his leg in two swings after that, figure we'd both wear a cast. The man screamed out in agony,

"You broke my leg! Oh my God! It's broken!"

"Cry me a river pretty boy, you don't see me complaining."

Finally I could leave in piece, I limped to the door. It felt like a muscle was pulled during the fight. Angel rushed to check on her level boyfriend first, but she abandoned him after I walked out the door. She ran after me shouting.

"Brian! Wait, Brian!"

I was curious what she had to say.

"What!?"

"Are you gone for good?"

I looked at her for a moment. She may have thought it was about her, but it wasn't. I was thinking that there was nothing here for me. My path was meant to be in KC, at least I could make sense of that world. There was a time where I could say the opposite, but things were different now.

Courtney was just outside of the house, parking her car. I just about missed her, she was wearing a low-cut blue dress. This of course to match her eyes, I had no time for her and wanted to leave.

"Hey!" She said, waving her arms franticly.

Courtney moved closer to talk to me, so I just went straight for the kiss. She was taken back, but kissed me back. As if I had just asked Angels permission and rushed to kiss the love of my life. Then I stopped and left her standing in place with her eyes closed. She only noticed that I walked away when my engine flared up.

"Brian! Where are you going?"

"Um, sorry! Just really got to poop."

Courtney dropped her face as she should have, on the spot I tried to think of an absurd reason for leaving that would distance her.

"Call me!" She yelled from afar.

That old truck ran smooth back to Derby, but it was ready to head towards Missouri. My siblings were awake when I went to get them, they were actually excited to go back to the city. We were gone for one day and everyone missed our new city lifestyle. My lip was the only physical sign that I had been in a fight. I hid the bruises and broken ribs from my siblings. They were surprisingly uninterested in my fight at Angel's house. I asked Vince if he wanted to know the story, he replied "You went to you ex's house, kind of expected this Brian." My sister asked a few questions about dad, but nothing about me. The trip was needed, but we rushed to leave Derby far behind us, never looking back.

Familiar Faces

Neither Vince nor Christy asked about Angel when we left. They didn't ask much of anything. Instead, they commentated on my fights in each fight night and how I could improve. They felt like I had a career in the ring, boxing for money. Vince discussed my weakness against a southpaw and the importance of cross training. Christy went into great detail about how I should move my feet when boxing. They were like two coaches who were mean as hell. It would be a long trip if I didn't steer the conversation away from scrutiny.

"Vince, did you pass out early at the party? I forgot to ask."

"At your birthday party? Took a nap pretty early, but after that I was up all night. Even after the magician showed up."

"What the hell? There was a magician?"

"Yeah, but he was super weird. He did street magic at like three in the morning. I left after he pulled out an Ouija board. "

"I thought that was a joke."

"Nope, it was one of the best nights of my life Brian."

Christy slapped my arm, she was seated in the middle of the pickup cab.

"Ask me what I did on your birthday Brian."

"Christy, what did you do on my birthday?"

"Well, I'm glad you asked. I binge watched two full seasons of my crime show & ate three pounds of cookie dough."

"Jeez, you guys had more fun than I did."

Vince began to laugh uncontrollably.

"Oh, you have no idea man. No idea at all."

"They were pretty loud Brian, I don't know how you didn't wake up." Christy added.

"Give me the full run-down Vince, what happened." I asked.

My little brother was excited to tell me all that he experienced that night. My stomach cringed at the thought of him doing drugs, especially hard drugs. I was hoping he knew better, plus Tanner didn't let people smoke anything but weed. That was a bonus to know he was strict on some things.

"Kendra, Candi & Luscious are all nerds. They were the coolest strippers I've ever met. " Vince said.

"You've met more strippers?" I asked, trying to keep my focus on the road.

"Of course, lots, anyways Candi is really good at first person shooters. She gave me tips that actually improved my game two fold!"

"That's it? Just improved your game?"

"Well, then we had some four-way action, but it only lasted a few hours before passing out."

"What?!" This was the story I wanted to know.

"Yeah Brian, they all got involved. Things got kind of dirty though when we split off into teams."

"Teams?"

"Well it was straight free-for-all at first, but then we had some split-screen action."

"Oh!" I said in my own realization. "You're talking about a video game."

"Uh, yeah, thought we were on the same page here?"

I chuckled. "We are now, sorry. My mind went south when you talked about strippers."

"Oh, well they showed me their boobs too, but that was later that night Brian."

My face dropped again. God, his life was so interesting to me. I knew he was downplaying the story to begin with.

"So why did it get loud then, Vince?"

He looked at me dismayed, clearly this was part of the story that he was less interested in.

"Well after the magician showed up, things got a little weird."

"Weird how Vince?"

"Well for starters, he told a bunch of people their fortunes, including me actually."

"What was yours?" Christy asked Vince.

"He said that I was the true heir & my blood was valuable." Vince replied.

"Are you being serious right now?" I asked my brother.

"Dude trust me, I'm not that creative. It really happened. Then things got weirder because he started throwing holy water on me, saying I was marked. I thought the whole thing was a joke until the house started shaking."

"Vince, that sounds like an exorcist."

"Whatever he was, he freaked me the fuck out! Tanner woke up & threw the guy out of the house. He said the guy must have been drunk or something, screaming at him in gibberish."

"Is that why you went to bed so late?" Christy asked.

"Yeah, I never really went back to sleep though. I just laid there thinking about the weird ass magician."

We mostly sat in silence from that moment, inside our own minds. I tried to bring up dad, but no one wanted to hear about him. Instead my siblings peered through the windshield, searching for their own answers.

The old truck pulled up to Tanner's place just after midnight. My siblings went straight to bed, while Tanner and I talked about the trip and what happened. After seeing I fought, he joked saying I was safer with him than at home. It was partly true, my grandfather was a bust and dad was out of the picture. The money that we earned was insurance. Anything that we saved could go towards staying off of the streets, worst case scenario I still have a truck.

He asked me about the trip & how things went with Angel. I told him about my father and the coffee shop & party. Tanner commented "Trouble follows you kid." Hate to say, but he was right. Everywhere I went seemed to have beef with me. Maybe I'm to blame, either way my conscious is clear.

Tanner must have known that preemptively that I would fail on my conquest. It was a lost hope from the start. Lance had already confirmed that my father was still gone & he knew Angel was promiscuous. Nonetheless I had to see her one last time, to finally let go of her.

I asked Tanner about the mysterious magician that had come to my birthday party. He seemed to brush it off easily. Saying that the guy showed up drunk and tried to scare all of the guests. The magician was three hours late and made everyone uncomfortable. Tanner was with a girl when things got out of hand. He kicked the magician out of the house half-naked.

"The guy was a loony kid, don't worry he won't be coming back."

He went to bed saying he had a surprise for me the next day, something to cheer me up. He kept me on my toes, never knowing what was coming next.

I laid in bed restless that night thinking about the future, maybe there was a business that we could start together. Kansas City was my kind of place anyways, it was a cocky city. It had drug use, prostitution, gang-violence, theft and assault in broad daylight. The things behind closed doors were darker, much darker.

The City was out of the limelight for the most part. Everyone knew Kansas City for the barbeque, the Royals and Chiefs for sports fans. Though the main action was underground, unknown to the public. There were mob ties all over the city, it was an unofficial crime city.

The following day Tanner drove me around for the next fight night location. We stopped at a tattoo shop in the corner of a strip mall downtown.

"What are we doing here?"

"Well, that's for you to decide."

"Really?"

"Yeah if you want. When I was heartbroken, once upon a time, I got inked. It was my way of saying, this is the 'new' me. She will never know this side of me."

"How many tattoos you got T?"

"Did you just call me T? I only have one, never get your heart broken more than once kid. That's a lesson you can take to the grave." Tanner shut off the engine to his car.

His words spoke volumes to me, without hesitation I replied.

"I know what I want."

"Well let's go then."

The place reeked of cigarettes and liquor. An old man covered in ink ran the shop, Tanner knew him since a boy. His name was Ronald, he had some of the thickest bifocals I'd ever seen. It made me slightly nervous that he had terrible eyesight. It's nothing something you want for your first tattoo. He went to shake my hand when he was introduced, but he missed my hand by at least a foot.

"Oops, sorry about that, my sight isn't what it used to be."

My mouth opened and I looked at Tanner with concern.

"He's good, trust me. Tell him what you want." He said.

I was reluctant for my first idea. It was an extravagant yoke that draped over my shoulders in three colors. That tattoo idea changed to two letters after meeting Ronald. I asked for "OX" in bold letters on my back, easy enough. It was my first time being in a tattoo chair, my expectations were low. I was okay with that though, I felt like part of the tribe having a tag on me.

Tanner watched and ate chips while I was in the chair. He lit a joint and passed it to Ronald while he was working on my back. After seeing my artist get high I became worried, Tanner insisted that I smoked to calm me down, but it wasn't for me. I turned away the joint and trusted he knew what he was doing. Then Ronald asked several bizarre questions and ranted about nonsense.

"Brian you ever wonder who would be at your funeral?"

"Like Tom Sawyer?"

"Who?" Ronald was confused.

"Like the book, you know?"

Ronald stopped tattooing and looked at me as if I were odd for referencing literature.

"Brain, don't tell me you're one of them people that reads for fun."

"No, well there's nothing really wrong with that, but no specifically to your question."

"Is he getting smart with me? It feels like he is." Ronald looked at Tanner for reassurance.

"No, he's just trying to be funny. He's cool man." Tanner passed Ronald the joint again.

"How high are you? This whole thing went from being fun to a nightmare."

"Now hold on youngster, you're going to like anything coming from these here hands I can promise you that. Now I'm going to take care of you, the smoke is just for pain."

We paused for a moment and I calmed down, "Okay, let's finish this thing then." I said, impatiently responding to Ronald's sass.

By the time he finished the two bold letters I asked for, three hours had passed. It irritated me at first, but the talent was in the line work in his tattooing. The two letters were perfectly square and equal to each other. On top of that, he free handed the piece so it was quite impressive. I judged Ronald too soon.

My upper back stung like I had been attacked by a swarm of bees. The entire ride back was agony leaned up against the seat of Tanner's Camaro. He told me that the pain was temporary and the ink was permanent. The sting was a reminder of self-progression, I was becoming a new person. It was hard to see where the road would take me from here. My path was unseen, only months ago I was beating nerds in chess. Now I'm in and an underground gambling arena, my ultimate goal changed.

"Tanner, how much would it cost to find into my father's attackers?"

He thought for a moment and gazed into the shadows for a moment.

"I'd say a few thousand if you want it done right. You'll need a private investigator and money to bribe witnesses for information."

"Done, I have the money saved for sure. I still want to find Slick, but I need to know why I'm here in the first place."

"I'm with you kid, but are you sure this is a road you want to go down? There is some vengeance at the end of that tunnel."

"Maybe I'm prepared for that, they have to pay for Eli. They took away my father, my life, everything. I have to know why or it will haunt me that they got away."

Tanner paused and exhaled deep in acceptance.

"Damn, okay. Well guess there is a manhunt out now, what could possibly go wrong?"

"Are you with me on this or not?"

"You don't even have to ask, you know the answer. I'm just scared of where your brother and sister will go."

Tanner went silent as we approached his house, he knew this would end in bloodshed.

The television was off when we returned home. Christy was reading on the couch in silence, Vince was doing sit-ups on the floor next to her. He had his head phones playing metal full blast.

"What's going on guys?" I couldn't wait to show off my tattoo.

"Brian!" Christy rose from the couch hugging me. Her hands grazed my fresh ink.

"Ow!" I jerked back, leaving her suspicious.

"What did I do?"

"Nothing I'm just a bit sore."

"Sore from what Brian?"

"Oh you'll see, I wanted to show you and Vince. What's he doing over there?"

"Um, working out obviously." Her eyes rolled at me.

"I can see that sis, why is he working out?"

"He says you don't have any abs and he can train to fight better than you."

"I do too have abs! They're just hiding right now."

Vince finished his workout and turned his music off.

"Brian, everyone knows you only run and shadowbox. You're neglecting a key point in your workout." Vince said.

"Oh yeah? And what am I missing?"

"The freaking workout!"

Tanner laughed hysterically from the kitchen, nosing in on the conversation.

"Ouch bro, damn it's a good thing I don't have feelings or anything."

"It's ok to be jealous Brian, check this out."

Vince pulls his shirt up to show me his six-pack of abs. He must have been at it for weeks, Vince was pretty chiseled, but I still had to down play my little brother.

"Holy crap Vince, do you eat anymore? I can see your ribs!"

Vince pulled his shirt back down as Christy giggled.

"Anyways I wanted to show you something bro."

I pulled my shirt up and turned around to reveal the artwork.

"Woah, I like it Brian, it makes you look older."

"Hugs and Kisses?" Vince guessed.

"That is 'XO' not 'OX' Vince." I pressed.

"Okay, so kisses and hugs then?"

"What? No! It says 'Ox' like the animal."

"Oh, yeah totally forgot dad gave you that necklace. Didn't think you would take it this far though."

"What the hell does that mean Vince?"

"Nothing, just saying you have two letters on your back now."

"You would've done differently?"

"Yeah, I mean for me it would be like an Ox pulling a cart of something heavy. That way you'd be like 'oh, that's an ox' Right?"

"Yeah I guess so, that sounds cool actually. Like maybe he is pulling the world, like he carries the weight of the world on his shoulders."

"Damn Brian you just got deep. The Ox carried the weight of the world on his shoulders. You just need to have the world on fire and you make it epic!"

I laughed at my judgmental brother, he actually hugged me and told me he thought it looked cool. Vince seemed happy for me, like he approved of who I was becoming. But he would still have to break balls now and again.

"Love yah, kid." I said to my brother, messing up his combed hair.

"Love you too." He replied.

"And me?" Christy asked.

"Of course, love you too sis."

"What is for dinner?" She said.

"We're having a family cookout tonight!" Tanner shouted from afar.

"What's the occasion?" Said Vince.

"Change!"

"Yikes, I better get ready." Christy said leaving me paranoid.

I noticed that she took better care of herself then she did in Derby. Christy was becoming a woman and I was not her mother or father. I could only hope that she made the right decisions, my heart couldn't bear a teen pregnancy situation. There would be consequences from her over protective older brother. Vince left to get ready as well, he knew that Tanner never had just a few people over.

I was expecting around twenty people max, but about forty showed up. I presented my fresh ink by wearing a tank-top like Tanners. Everyone asked about it and loved the story behind my mother's gift. The atmosphere was that of a family reunion, everyone had a good time. Spanish brought tamales that were unbelievably spicy, but irresistible. It was a bit cliché.

Lance showed up with four girls that I suspected loved cocaine. They were sure outsiders but everyone looked away. Tanner knew that Lance had them under control, or he would leave.

Drew was a local fight night fighter that showed up with his kids. They ran wild and Drew didn't care at all. He ignored them like they were not his children. The little ones were becoming destructive, so Christy helped manage the chaos. She took them to the basement and started a pretend daycare. Putting on cartoons and playing games.

Victor, one of the winners from fight night was there with his wife. The guy from the corner store showed up eating a hot dog covered in mustard. There was Dre the fighter and his family. Several of the ring girls also came. The entire cookout party was comprised of Tanner's circle for the most part, feeling like a family. I made my way around the cookout greeting everyone.

"What up Spanish you good?"

"You already know Ox!"

"Hey you're the first one to get it right."

I turned to the girls who stood with Lance.

"How's it going ladies you having fun?"

The snowed out blondes with Lance nodded and carried on.

"How you doing Lance?"

"Oh, good brotha, living the dream."

"That's what I like to hear."

A random man with glasses approached me.

"What up Brian, badass burgers."

"Thanks, Tanner made them enjoy."

"Will do Ox."

I didn't know the guy, but I liked that the name caught on. People called me something that stood for might or strength.

Outside was a different feeling, less people and calmer. I opened a beer and joined Tanner by the grill. There was nothing but love in the house and chill vibes. Until a brief moment where we received an unwanted guest.

Out of the corner of my eye I saw a shadow approach the fence.

"Quite the party you got going on here." A deep voice said.

"Get out of here eight ball! You're not welcome here."

"Oh, you've made that perfectly clear now haven't you? No harm Tanner, right now I want to talk to your brother over here."

"You have words for me?"

"More than that, you'll find out. For now, I just wanted to let you know I'll be seeing you real soon."

"Is that a promise?" I taunted.

He chuckled. "You aren't so big boy, I'd keep my mouth shut if I was you."

"If you knew how 'big' I was you would keep your mouth open."

Eight ball paused and laughed understanding my foul joke. He turned and walked away.

"Be seeing you boys around."

This put me on edge knowing that he was waiting for me. I put him down once, but would I be so lucky as to do it twice? Tanner carried a gun with him, but I only had my knuckles for my saving grace. The one thing I did know was that he would be looking for me to slip up. My guess is that he wanted me in a body bag, but I always stayed in a group in mostly crowded areas.

He wouldn't dare cross Tanner. It would bring the entire block against him. No way was eight ball that dumb, at least I gave him enough credit for that. I would just be extra cautious from now on, always peering over my shoulder knowing there is a target on my back.

"Should I be worried?" I asked Tanner.

"No, but you shouldn't be taunting the guy either. You got enough enemies kid."

He was right & the list was growing. I had Angels ex and his friends, the local gangs, eight-ball, and my father's attackers all as foes. It was beginning to bother me, I needed to get my mind off of such things and enjoy the party. Tanner had the perfect person in mind for the job. He received a text from his cousin who was at the front door.

"Come meet someone real quick Brian."

I followed Tanner to the door where a beautiful dark haired girl with hazel eyes waited.

"Ashley, this is my friend Brian we talked about."

"Hi, it's nice to meet you. You can just call me Ash."

Instantly it was lust at first sight, I could not even picture Angels face at that moment. Ashley had me so taken back my senses were gone.

"Right on, you can just call me Brian. I mean, call me whatever."

We shared a moment where we starred into each other's eyes. I wanted her to know I was deeply interested in her, Tanner was quick to notice.

"Wow, anyways I'm going to leave you two kids alone to get to know each other. Have fun!"

As the night carried on people trickled off, leaving close to dark. Only a few stuck around to play pool or drink with a buddy. Victor ended up crashing on the couch after pissing off his old lady. She was his ride home. He said it was typical for a Friday night.

I stayed up most of the night talking to Ashley. She was Tanners first cousin thorough his aunt on his mother's side. She was hard working, she was in school working towards her bachelorette in music. She wanted to be a musician, but changed to teaching music instead. Her work schedule was crazy too, she had a full time job on top of her education.

She hasn't seen Tanner in years and he invited her to the cookout. He probably knew that I would like her for two reasons. One, she was unbelievably gorgeous, and two she listened. She was caught up on my life story & I listened to hers. We never really went to sleep, we just cuddled in place on the couch talking all night.

Around five or six in the morning I finally dozed off and gave in to sleep deprivation. Ashley was gone when I woke up in the afternoon. She left a note next to my pile of drool beside my face. It read:

Brian, had a great time last night. We should do it again soon.

Xoxo--> OX

She was great, I couldn't wait to see her again and we didn't
have sex. Hell we didn't kiss either, Ash and I just cuddled but it
meant something. It felt like she was a girl worth working for,
also I would officially be in the Brady family if it worked out.

Vince was sparing with Spanish in the living room wearing boxing
gloves. I didn't want my brother fighting in a competition like me,
but it was his choice. We had refs and head gear, I knew first
hand that it was overly safe. If anything the fight experience
would protect Vince, if he ever gets into that situation. It is a
tough world out there and you have to survive by any means
necessary. This was my way of allowing my brother to learn for
himself as well as give him discipline.

Christy took on painting, she always wanted to paint on a canvas
but never did. Tanner bought her a paint by number to help
practice and she used it often. She wanted to learn how to paint
puppies, that was her favorite thing in the world. More than
chocolate, Christy loved puppies.

"Looks good Christy, what is it going to be?"

"This one is of a mountain peak in the winter."

I perched over the semi blank outline on the canvas.

"Oh, yeah. I can kind of see it."

"It's making me freaking cold but, I'm learning a lot."

"Good, I can't wait to see it."

"Well hopefully I can fix it, I made the clouds too dark."

"That's okay, we learn through our mistakes."

Christy looked towards the ceiling in thought.

"Hmm, guess you're right. You can't change what's meant to happen."

I kissed my sister on the head, then ruffled up her hair with my palm.

"Ugh, Brian!"

"Love yah!" I said running out of the room.

Tanner had already arranged me a second date with his cousin. He planned on taking the entire family to the Kansas City Market that weekend. It was the off-week of fight night and the weather was perfect for an outing.

It was like everything that we went through came back to us in a positive way. My father was in the hospital, but my family was never closer. Couldn't find my grandfather, but I found a new brother. Lost love in Angel but gained it back in Ashley. My new high on life gave me the inspiration to suggest a business plan to Tanner

After dinner that night I took Tanner outside and proposed a plan to legitimize the business.

"What's this all about B?" He asked me.

"I want to grow the business." I said raising my hands in excitement.

"You got my attention."

"What about us going legitimate?"

"In fighting?"

"Yeah, like we make a boxing tournament legally."

"Already tried B."

"Really?" I said in a high pitch voice.

"Yeah Brian, if everything were that simple I'd already have my own gym and events. You jump through hoops and all the profits are taken. Fuck that! I'd rather do it my way and have fun before everything comes crashing down."

"You think so?"

"Oh yeah bro, for sure. Everyone goes down one day. At least I know my day is coming."

"Damn."

"What?" Tanner asked concerned.

"I just want to be part of things you know? Like I thought that if we expanded that I would be involved."

"Brian you are part of things, don't you see that?"

"Well yeah, but I want to help."

"Dude, you do plenty. Just take it one day at a time brother. Who knows, your dad might wake up next week. Then it's back to school for you and you forget all about me."

"No I won't! I could never forget what you did for us Tanner."

"Not like that B, I'm just saying to take things easy. You don't know if we both die tomorrow, so why worry about it? For me, I only live for the day. If the day goes how I wanted, then that day is won. You have to win each day, fuck tomorrow. Did you do what you wanted to today?"

"Well I wanted some chips."

Tanner laughed at my ill-timed joke. "Shut up Brian, you're becoming an asshole like Vince. But hey, I still love you kid."

He smacked me twice lightly on the cheek like a mobster.

I was taking things too fast, always wanting more. Someone in a comma could awake in months, I didn't give Eli enough time. It was wrong for me to plan the rest of my life, without waiting for my father.

Cause & Effect

That Friday night Tanner took me to meet someone that he knew, he was a local celebrity that bought Tanner's finest crop. He was an exclusive customer that was loyal to the marijuana that Tanner grew. On the drive over to the celebrity's house Tanner told me that the guy was an underground legend. He was the rap king of KC, and went by Tech. Tanner knew him by a different name however. We pulled up to a gated house with a camera attached to it. Tanner pushed a small red button that ring the doorbell to an unknown voice. I assumed a butler of some kind as he was described.

"Who is it?" A voice asked with an aggressive tone.

"Yeah, it's Tanner. Here to see Aaron."

Buzz, then the door slid open and Tanner pulled to the front. The house was two stories and not as impressive as the security system. It was as if he upgraded his childhood house to the max. Installing a giant fence with grand landscaping after fame. He probably bought the adjoining lot and demolished the property for a bigger yard. For Kansas City, inner city, the lot was huge.

As we approached the front door it opened automatically. Someone was waiting for us behind the door, to Tanner this was normal.

We were instructed that Tech was recording, we waited outside the studio for him to finish. After about twenty minutes of watching this guy record, he finally came out to greet us. He looked different from typical rappers. Tech didn't wear gold chains or fancy jewelry, his shoes were white as snow though. Very well kept, his clothes looked new and pressed. He was a middle aged black man with a long braded beard. His hair braided down the back of his head like a Mohawk. Tech was nostalgic about seeing Tanner, he greeted him coming out of the recording booth.

"Brady! As I live and breathe, how you doing brother?"

"Good, staying active, you know." Tanner said with a smile.

"Brady?" I said questioning.

"Yeah, we go back. Like two hand tag-team football back in the day." Tech replied.

"Tech, I want you to meet a close friend of mine Brian Vega." Tanner introduced us.

Tech shook my hand vigorously.

"Call me Aaron, pleased to meet you Brian."

I had pictured Tech having a different real name than Aaron. Something more aggressive, but he seemed humble.

"You guys want to hear a fresh track?" Tech asked us.

"Hell yeah!" Tanner sputtered.

He had a thousand buttons with different lights on a mixing board. I was impressed that Tech knew what to press and how to use the giant machine. Most people required a special technician for mixing.

He played us a song that he had been working on for a month. It was insane, I couldn't keep up with the lyrics because of the speed. The sound was addicting though, it was a new a way to speak for the people through lyricism. He was a master at assembling words together and it showed in his music. Before Tanner introduced him, I had never heard of Tech. He played mainly rap music at the house but it was outside my norm. My father raised us listening to gospel music or classic rock. The music that Tech made was so different from anything I had been exposed to.

He might have made my acquaintance that day, but he also gained a fan. When the song ended he genuinely eager for feedback.

"So what-cha think?"

"That shit hits a mad note, dope as fuck." Tanner said.

"Yeah, Tech I loved too." I added.

"Aaron." He corrected.

"Oh, sorry Aaron. I'll remember it."

"It's all good, see me in concert and scream Tech. But here I'm just Aaron though."

"Damn, I like that."

He seemed to be a modest man who loved music, I wished more artists were like him.

"Yo Tanner, you got something for me?"

Aaron looked at Tanner sitting in an office chair and smiled.

"Now you know I make house visits."

Tanner stood up and pulled out a sack of herb from his pants pocket. He had already ground up the bud and syphoned it for imperfections.

"This is a sativa called Murphy's child, and in my other pocket I have a hybrid."

Tanner was proud of his skill growing the plants.

"What's the hybrid you brought?" Aaron asked.

"Glad you asked my boy, this here is my pride and joy." He handed Aaron the bag. "This one is called Sour-Widow, it's definitely a creeper."

"Sold, hook me up with both. What's the damage?"

"Friend range is at least a buck-twenty, but you're family Aaron. So it's a 'G' solid today." Tanner said, charging him only a thousand dollars.

"Somebody please pay this man." Aaron shouted holding his new purchase.

A figure from the corner of the room shuffled over and handed Tanner a stack of cash. Well over a thousand, Aaron knew how to treat his friends. This was considered a tip of sorts for services rendered. Tanner had painstakingly cultivated his product months for this moment. Each bag that he carried was over two ounces a piece. Together it weighted just over a quarter pound. Aaron was aware of Tanners dedication, thus he rewarded him.

"Okay, so before you leave you got to hit this."

Aaron rolled a cigar filled with the newly purchased green. He fired up the end and toked down before passing it to Tanner. They both smoked with such ease it was scary almost. One hit was all it took to have me coughing on the floor.

Tanner and Aaron continued smoking and talking while I stared at the ceiling. I was contemplating life and the meaning of happiness. It had not occurred to me that I was high as hell at the time. I could still hear Tanner and Aaron chatting through my hazy clouds. Crazy thing is, I thought that they sounded high on drugs, not me. Ignoring the fact I was lying on the ground talking to myself.

"You still do that fight night?" Aaron asked.

"Oh yeah, but it's grown quite a bit since you've been there."

"No doubt, need to stop by the old stomping grounds."

"You're always welcome." Tanner whispered, his voice changed pitch at inopportune moments.

"Is he one of your lost boys?"

Tanner laughed knowing he saves the misguided. "Guess you can say that." He looked at Tech seriously for a moment and called in a well-deserved favor.

"Maybe you can help me out with something."

"Anything." Aaron said.

Tanner continued. "Does the name Ignacio Vega mean anything to you?"

"No, but it sounds familiar. You looking for this guy?"

"Well, it's complicated, but that's the kid's grandfather."

"Oh I see I'll get someone to look into it for you."

They continued smoking until reaching my elevation. Then laughter spread like wild fire between the two. That was the last thing I remembered before being woken up by Tanner to go back home. The floor had provided a facilitating bed for at least an hour.

I was still slightly buzzed on the way home. Tanner seemed un-phased, ready for the rest of the night. I had forgotten about the Kansas City market in the morning and the date with Ashley. The only thing on my mind was spreading out on my bed.

I awoke Saturday morning & everyone was ready to go to the Kansas City Market. It was nearly ten o'clock and I slept like a baby. Christy was not feeling well, she said that she was vomiting the night before. I felt terrible and wanted to stay behind and help. She insisted we leave without her and have fun. She said that she didn't feel like being around people anyways and would probably just sleep all day. She was surrounded by weapons in a house with thirteen locks, so I felt safe about leaving her alone.

Ashley was going to meet us there, she lived on the nice side of town towards the Kansas state line. I threw on a dark blue button-up collared shirt and jeans. Trying to dress casual but classy, Tanner and Vince looked normal. Vince with his endless set of polos and Tanner with his white tank-top. We left Christy and gave her an eta of two hours being gone. Ashley was running late, so Tanner, Vince and I got cream cheese filled croissants. They were incredible, warm and locally made. We went back for a second one after devouring our first.

When Ash showed up it was worth the wait, she was all dolled-up. Heavy on the mascara and light on the clothing. The only thing to keep my mind at bay was the amazing food offered at the market. Otherwise I'd be staring at her the entire time.

There were stalls for just about everything. Ashley wanted to see kittens first, so we went to the animal side of the market. Vince was more interested in the video game inspired stalls, so he split up with Tanner. It was summertime, but Ashley took online courses in college. The classes took most of her free time, so the market was a nice break from reality.

At the time all I wanted to do was hold her hand, so I made the move. Ashley reciprocated with a kiss on the cheek. The simple gesture was cute and resembled her personality. She was a girl that I wanted to be around, one that I wanted to keep. We talked about family and the future. All she ever wanted was to be a nurse and work in the delivery room. After school she was ready to start a family and slow down the ambition. She was young and driven, I liked that about her.

 The Kansas City Market had something for everyone. There were areas for guns and ammo, or there was grain sold by the pound. Anyone from the city could technically rent a booth so the options were limitless. We met up with Tanner and Vince who carried full bags of accessories and video games. I hoped that he didn't just spend our entire savings as if it he were on a sponsored shopping spree.

We congregated to the food court and ate corndogs, funnel cake, and turkey legs. It felt like being at the fair, only lacking the rides and games. Vince showed me a sweater he bought for Christy, it was very girly, perfect for her. His thoughtfulness caused me to get some food to-go for her as well. She was sick, but maybe her appetite would return.

We parted ways with Ashley mid-afternoon. She returned home and we headed back to our corner of the city. My appreciation for the city grew that day, there was a side that I hadn't seen. There was a culture that surrounded great food, they prided themselves on it. Barbeque was running through the veins of the people who lived there. I was happy to be part of the experience.

Tanner messed with me a bit on the ride home, he cracked jokes about his cousin. He told me her father was a cop. He then corrected snickering saying the man was a senator. Vince caught on and teased that her father was racist, but it came across ill-tempered. He proceeded to explain his jest, even though the moment had passed for laughter.

There were flashing lights at both ends of Tanner's street. Close to his house was an ambulance parked outside and a fire truck.

"Woah, what the hell happened here?" Tanner said.

We pulled closer to the house and into the driveway. I noticed that the police were interviewing the neighbors. Then a sickening pain shot through my stomach, what if it was us? The car came to a stop and a police officer walked out of Tanners house.

"What the fuck?" Tanner exclaimed in curiosity.

"Christy!" I said soaring out of the car.

The officer by Tanners house tried to stop me but I rushed past him into the house. Where was my little sister? Why did the police come? I had to find her.

"Christy!" I ran to the basement checking her room. There was no sign of her. "Christy! Sis! Where are you?" my heart accelerated past reckoning. The feeling left me breathless and dazed falling to the floor panting.

"Brian." I heard in the commotion. The voice brought me to my feet, it could have been her. I crawled back upstairs to hear the voice call again, this time much clearer.

"Brian!" Vince yelled running to my aid. "Are you ok?"

"Christy, where is she?" I mumbled through broken breath. He wrapped my arm around his neck as a crutch.

"Alright come-on Ox, you have to help me here. She's outside, she needs you right now."

I gained my composure and came to my senses, I rushed to find her outside the front door. She must have been next door when something happened I thought.

Walking outside revealed the world. Tanner was next to the ambulance talking to an officer. Spanish was next to him beat to a pulp. He leaned next to Tanner distraught, then it hit me. Christy was in the ambulance and Spanish must have known something. I stumbled down the stairs nearly busting my face open to see inside the vehicle.

When I saw her state I lost my composure and vomited next to the truck. They had hurt my baby, what did they do to her? She was so sweet and innocent, she wouldn't hurt a fly. Who would do this? I deserved answers. My sister was on a breathing tube going to the hospital after who knows what happened to her. Before my rage aimed at Spanish, Tanner explained the situation.

"Hold up Brian." He said putting his hand on my chest. "Spanish protected her. That's why he looks like this."

I calmed down realizing my gratitude should be directed at Spanish.

"You have my statement, can you give us a moment?" He said in a condescending tone at an officer. "Spanish, tell Brian what you told me." Tanner said.

The policeman gave us space while the situation was explained.

"It was eight-ball B. He says he got permission to take out your whole family."

I was stunned by his statement. "Permission from who?"

"He didn't say. He just said that your pops wasn't in an accident, it was a hit."

"Why were you here in the first place?"

"Well um⋯" Spanish hesitated to tell me the truth.

"Spit it out!"

"Christy invited me over to hang out, she faked being sick."

That statement hit me hard, not only did she lie but she also liked boys. I wasn't used to her developing to a state that left teenage boys speechless. She was my sissy, my little buddy that was sweeter than sugar.

"That's big news Brian." Tanner said of the darkness of my mind.

"How so?"

"Because, eight-ball knows about your family. How else would he get permission to wipe out everyone?"

My knuckles were clinched tight, I wanted to rush off and hurt the man behind this attack. I knew who eight-ball was, he would pay. My entire bloodline was in jeopardy and I knew nothing of the origin. It would become my mission to seek out the hunter and destroy the threat. My rage was unbearable, but Vince stopped me. Christy needed me by her side, which is where I belonged. Vince and I rode with her to the hospital, holding her hands.

"I'll meet you guys there!" Tanner yelled running to start his car with Spanish next to him.

The EMT slammed the doors and rushed us off to the hospital. Vince held Christy's hand while I laid my head by her feet weeping. Tanner drove like a madman following the ambulance to the hospital, as though he attained a special license to be reckless. I noticed my sister's hand returning the squeeze to my little brother. He sang to her a song that my mother sang to us a children. Vince brushed her hair crying with full bodied emotion. It was hard to see him so broken.

Spanish said that my predator wanted the whole family dead. That echoed through my mind on a repeating score. Did my father know of this threat? If so, was he protecting us from someone all along? There were too many unanswered questions.

I thought my life was interesting for being part Irish mixed with Mexican and Italian. To me that would carry a story with higher ups and less falls. Real life is cruel to a world that struggles to cope without warmth in their hearts. Like such an atrocity of hurting my sister, he struck at the heart. Eight-ball was calling me out, he wanted to toy with my mind and destroy my life. Who knows how long he actually stalked my every movement to find weakness.

Arriving at the hospital the staff rushed my sister away and separated Vince and me to the waiting area. Tanner was already there, the ambulance must have been to slow for him. He was deeply concerned as well.

"Did that say anything?" Tanner asked as we sat down.

"Not yet." Said Vince. "She is conscious though."

"Spanish, what else happened?"

"Well, they jumped me when I was going into the house and knocked my ass out cold."

"So you didn't see what happened to her?" I was concerned that his filthy hands touched her.

"No, but I saw her after they left."

"Did she say anything?"

"Nah, I called nine-one-one immediately."

"When did he tell you about my family?"

"After stomping my ribs, what you want from me?"

"I'm sorry, this shit is just heavy."

"Trust, I want this cat dead. You may not believe this, but I really have feelings for Christy."

I peered through his remark and disregarded his adolescence. He had good intentions and attempted to protect her diligently. As for love, it is not without pain. He may have felt this way once defending her honor.

If only I had been there to give eight-ball what he needed. A reminder that he was beaten before and can be again. He may have towered over me, but it would not stop me from tearing him apart limb from limb. I demanded retribution for Christy, this was too far.

Hurt me, hell kill me even, but never lay a hand on my sister.

The waiting room grew as time went on with no answer. My sister had a strong handful of men ready to fight for her. Lance, Victor and several of the fight night guys came out. Even a former competitor who was recently injured, Cody. Some of the ring girls found out what happened and brought Christy a gift basket. Everyone was so nice and supportive.

Victor gave me his word that he would fight by my side against eight-ball. Hurting a kid in the neighborhood meant big trouble. Not just with the law, the streets had its own way of handling offenders. People were out looking for him on both sides of the law. He was hiding out with someone who protected him. Possibly the person who gave the permission of my families' termination. Then a figure from my past appeared from thin air, it was Angel. She was looking for Christy, after word reached her.

"What are you doing here?"

"Saw it on the news, I came as soon as I could."

"You watched the news in Wichita and saw a story here?"

"Yeah, it was brief but I saw Christy's face."

"When the hell were there news cameras?" Vince asked rhetorically.

"Oh, they get the hell out of the ghetto after the story." Victor added.

"Is it okay that I'm here?" Angel said.

"Of course, Christy would want you here."

She gave me a hug and squeezed tight.

"Oh Brian, this is terrible, I miss your family so much."

"Miss you too Angel!" Vince shouted from his seat, ease dropping.

"Have a seat." I said, ignoring her words of endearment.

She smiled and I introduced her to Tanner. We were broken, but we were together. Who knows if I could get through this alone? Angel's face was warming, she reminded me of my father and the way things used to be. I did miss Angel, but she needed freedom and I was happier with Ashley.

A doctor came and gave me her status in person, trying to be discrete about certain parts. Her jaw was broken in two places, she had a fractured rib on both sides. She had to have stiches on her forehead and lip. The man then informed me that he found skin under her nails and she allowed a rape test administered.

She gave her statement to police before receiving pain killers. The doctor told me that Christy could have visitors, but be distant as she is injured. I was the first to visit and promised a quick return to swap with someone else.

Christie was still beautiful through the battle wounds. She struggled and gave the cops something to take him down. My sister was stronger than I was. She was conscious and fully aware after being pumped full of painkillers.

"Hey sis." I said entering the room, she was expecting me.

"You're not the only fighter in the family you know."

I smiled and kissed her on the top of her head.

"I'd rather you fight in the ring to be honest."

Christy chuckled and yawned. It was probably a very long day for her and she was still in good spirits.

"Who brought the candy?" She asked pointing at a gift basket.

"That's from Stephanie the ring girl."

"Maybe because I gave her my zucchini bread recipe."

"Seriously?"

"Yeah, why?"

"She is a ring girl sis, who knows what she does for a real job. She could be selling our family recipes."

"Steph strips for her other job Brian, you're silly. That is where Tanner met her, a strip club."

I remembered how brutally honest Christy is and how she didn't see barriers between class.

"Never mind that, what matters is that you are safe now." I said.

My hand reached to touch my sister's leg to reassure her. She flinched before I touched her. My hand retracted and my eyes quivered away. Eight-ball must have robbed my sister of her innocence. It might damage her for the rest of her life, something that she carries with her. My sister's poor sweet soul, I couldn't dare tell my father, let alone another human being. Faking strength for Christy was lost. This broke me, but I couldn't let her see. She had to know that her brother was strong for her.

My sister extended her arms for an embrace.

"Slowly, I'm sore." Christy said.

I cried on my sisters shoulders. It was my job to be her protector and I failed. My body was overcome with emotion for my beloved.

"I'm so sorry sis, I should have been there."

"It's okay Brian, look I'm still alive. He didn't kill me."

"I know, but it is my fault you are here."

She rubbed my back to comfort me.

"Hey, I don't blame you Brian. I could never blame you. Don't do that to yourself. If anything it's my fault for staying behind."

I stopped sobbing and looked my sister straight in her eyes.

"It is not your fault either, not at all!"

She grabbed my shoulders. "Brian, it is no one's fault, let the police handle things."

"Hmm." I turned away.

"Brian, seriously no more trouble. It ends with me."

"I love you, I'll send Vince in next."

My frustration with morals grew at that moment. I did not want to hear from anyone who opposed my retribution. Eight-ball would pay in full, I left the room and continued to the waiting room.

"How is she?" Tanner asked.

"Better than I thought, but worse than she should be."

"You got that right."

"Can I go in now?" Vince asked.

"Yeah, she is waiting on you."

My little brother left to see Christy in her room. I was still on edge pacing back and forth. Suddenly Victor spoke up after receiving a text.

"Hey someone saw eight-ball down on Independence."

Without a moment's notice I jolted out of the room.

"Shit!" Tanner said chasing me.

The entire room followed me to find eight-ball. A village of angry commoners with pitch forks and torches. I wanted blood, they wanted a show. I ran to Tanners car to the driver side and yelled to him.

"Keys!" He threw them at me and I turned over the engine.

Tanner barely made it into the car before I took off in a rage. Lance followed behind with a group and Victor with another.

"Brian, don't you think this might be a set up? He wants you to come after him!"

I ignored Tanners rational and pressed the pedal to the floor whizzing through traffic at high speeds. Cops were not on my radar, just bloodthirsty vengeance. My visions of execution were endless, he would meet my full potential unfiltered. Trap or no trap I was coming for him. The car stereo blared the mixtape that

Tech gave to Tanner. For some reason the music helped me concentrate. My complete focus was on finding him. I looked down Independence till Tanner pointed at eight-ball's car outside of a pool hall.

He was right, it felt like a trap. Things felt weird the moment I put the car in park, I could see eight ball through the window. Tanner and I walked towards the pool hall. It just didn't feel right, cheese on a mousetrap. People seemed to be staring at us from the adjacent buildings. The news stand salesmen went stiff, cars drifted away.

Eight-ball had some outside help, the whole block was like a façade. Everyone seemed to be faking what they were doing, while watching us. I looked over my shoulder realizing I was several yards away from the car. Tanner took my que I gave him. We ran to the car as fast as possible to escape, but it was too late.

The ambush had already began. I heard the sound multiple gunshots without knowing where it came from. Then several shots were fired from multiple locations. Inside and outside buildings. We came from the hospital unarmed, I led basically Tanner to our death. He and I ran to find cover, each dodging bullets as they whizzed past our heads.

"Brian, we have to get the hell out of here!"

"How? They have us all jammed up!"

Then the Calvary arrived. Victor, Lance, Spanish and six others jumped out of their vehicles shooting. Lance was the only one who had to get out of his car and go to his trunk for the gun. He walked slowly to his popped trunk as if he wasn't being shot at, he ran on his own time.

"Gun! Someone give me a piece!" Tanner yelled.

Everyone looks at each other thinking another person will step up. No one rose to the occasion to help Tanner with a weapon.

"Really? Not one person brought an extra gun? Tell me you guys have more than one clip."

Again everyone who showed up realized simultaneously that they have limited ammo in a gunfight. They look at each other at first to confirm, suddenly the help became frugal with their cover fire.

"You got to be kidding me. We're dead, we are fucking dead. Sorry Brian, but revenge ends here kiddo."

"Tanner, we have to get inside!"

"What? No! Why?"

"That building has a fire alarm, if we pull it···"

"Then someone comes, good idea Brian! You do that and I'll stay here."

Tanner pulled out a mini-pistol from his pant leg and shot towards eight-ball's crew.

"Are you serious? You had that the whole time?"

"I forgot! Sorry! Go! Three minutes Brian!"

One of Eight-ball henchmen had a rail gun or heavy machine gun. It ripped holes through both sides of our protecting vehicles. The bullets killed several of our guys instantly. Cars exploded around us like an action movie. They were turned to ash before my eyes. Glass rained down from the sky dusting the air with particles of debris. Tanner unloaded his magazine trying to take out the machine gun man, he succeeded shooting him in the temple. The moment he fired, I ran inside, within seconds I found the fire alarm and pulled it to call for help. I rushed back to the entrance but was caught off guard.

"Where you going?" Eight-ball said.

He hit me in the jaw and I lost my balance.

"You know I'm actually going to enjoy this."

Eight-ball hit me again knocking me to the ground. My life was on the line, I had to fight for it. His strikes were brutal, I could not suffer too many blows before being unconscious. It was time to act on my fight training, move my feet, jive my skull. Give him a hard target, this was after all only one man.

I gained my composure and lifted my hands to defend myself properly. He swung on me but missed, I shook him. Again and again, duck, jive, jab. There was a rhythm to my moves, I had a song playing in my head. He couldn't him me and I was slowly causing damage with my one-two jab combos. He ate every one of my punches and became irritated charging me, he tackled me into the wall and lifted me off of the ground. Then he used his momentum and forced me to the ground. He wrapped his palms tightly around my neck with intention to kill.

"See boy! You know how to box, but not on the streets."

I struggled to get him off of me before I passed out. My hands reached to the sides of me looking for a weapon. I felt a shard of broken glass, it slit my hand to grasp, but was worth the pain. I jammed it into the side of his leg and broke off the excess. He was still on top of me, but he released my neck and grabbed thigh. I gasped for air, coming back to my full senses. Seeing weakness I jabbed several times at his abdomen, then striking his leg forcing the glass further inward. He screamed in agony falling to my side on the ground. Quickly I sprang to my feet.

"I know street, but you don't know intelligence!"

I kicked him several times while he was downed. He was done, there wasn't any fight in him left.

"I never want to see you here again. Get the hell out of town or I'll kill you! That's not a threat, it's a promise."

Out of spite I punted my foot across his face. My crew was downed outside, the importance of revenge fell from my list. I jogged to see the damage of the fallen. There was no sound of shooting, the air filled with the scent of blood. Coming into light the dead became clear. We had casualties on both sides, Victor and two other fighters were laid out on the ground lifeless. Tanner and Lance were huddled around Spanish who was bleeding out. He had been shot multiple times and started to become pale.

"Just hold on Johnny, help is almost here." Lance whispered to Spanish while stroking his hair. He could hear the ambulance in a distance knowing seconds were precious.

Tanner looked away from Spanish and rested on my shoulders fighting the urge to cry. He regained his composure and looked around for how close help was.

"Brian." Spanish said.

"What is it kid?" I stooped to his level so he could save his energy.

"Tell Christy I love her, I don't think I'll ever get the change to tell her." Spanish smiled holding my hand with his fist drenched in blood. Then I felt him pass, he released his final breath on this world.

Lance screamed "No! Come on Johnny, come back to me." He slammed on his chest to attempt revival.

Tanner finally gave into his emotions. He felt guilty and put his hand over his mouth. Tanner could not believe that Spanish was gone. It was too soon, he should have stayed behind.

"He was just a kid you know?" Tanner said. "His blood is on my hands now."

Words could not express how he felt and I couldn't comfort him. His death was my fault just as much as Tanner's. The Fire truck pulled around the corner trying to get through the brigade of cars. The driver was not prepared for the carnage that had just ensued. The police officers and ambulance would be only seconds behind them. It felt like everything I had been part of had come to an end.

Then the devil spoke to me from a distance, it was eight-ball back for more. Out of the corner of my eye I could see a gun pointed at my back.

"Did she tell you she liked it? Bet your sister kept that shit a secret huh? Yeah, see I'm going to clip you, then your brother. But not your sister, nah I got plans for her. Might just keep her around to let everyone get a taste."

His words pierced through me and I rushed towards him he shot at me and missed. Then again he aimed proper made a direct hit. My adrenaline did not allow me to stop, I continued and pursued his weapon kicking it out of his hands. Never have I trained my kicks for fighting but it came natural. The gun flew away and I seized the moment slamming my skull into his face.

He fell, then my arms fired like cannons, repeatedly smashing his face in. The fight gave out, he was unconscious and not moving. I could not stop though, my rage was too strong. I could not see that he was far past dead and I pounded away at his body. Seeing red, over and over I purged.

Finally my senses returned to me and I was aware of my surroundings again. My knuckles were bloody, there might have been a couple bullets logged in me and my face was rearranged. There was a crowd of people surrounding me, they starred at the bodies from the bloody aftermath. Some started to take photos, clearly I had taken a life, but he would never touch my sister again.

Again out of spite I hit eight-ball's body.

Someone would pay for the mess, but in that moment all I wanted was a smoke. After I finished one I finally heard it.

"Freeze, Don't move scumbag!" An officer said.

Oh great the hero's in blue, I'm sure that they will find a way to infect my wounds. I complied and put my hands on my head, but they threw me to the ground and bent my arm high behind my back. The handcuffed everyone with a pulse and carefully watched those without one.

Consequences

After the massacre in Kansas City people were on edge. The average person heard about the story through the news and related it to gang violence. The public was told to stay indoors late at night and make sure to lock the door.

The truth was far from that, a story no one would believe anyways. A tale of an assassination attempt on the prince of a mobster's empire. I did not know the full story myself and wanted answers sitting in a jail cell.

It was hard for any crime to be connected because of poor interrogations. No one talked, we knew better. All for one is what we thought about, let them piece the shit together on their own. Tanner was let loose due to the lack of evidence. He was good at finding loopholes in the system. Lace was set free because he could not be linked either. He was just trying to protect Spanish, the police saw his side.

As for me I had bullet wounds that needed to be tended to first. My assumption from movies was, I go to the hospital first. In my case they took me to the hospital in handcuffs. After stiches and bandages I was immediately processed and sent off to county jail to await my trial. They took my finger prints and mugshot and strip searched me. My bail was set at fifty thousand dollars, with an early trial. I was going to need one hell of a lawyer to get out of this one.

For the first time I felt completely alone, everyone was gone. I had no idea about Christy, Vince or Angel, completely cut off from the outside world. The cells were dim and cold, I had imagined having my own cell. In my head there were two sets of bunkbeds in each cell. Allowing for around four inmates maximum. That was way off, I was led into a giant room filled with men. Most of which probably committed a violent crime such as myself.

As I was led to my bunk, inmates shouted and starred. They called me a string full of names including "Fresh meat." Which I felt rather gross about and "Cod fish" which I had no idea what it meant. There were maybe one hundred and fifty to two hundred men in my block. The jail had four blocks total, all with a different letters to signify the severity of crime.

The first block "A" was for those of smaller crimes, unpaid parking tickets. Mostly non-violent crimes. I was in block "D" were they put the rapists, seral killers and psychos before trial. For months now I had been fighting to survive, just trying to stay alive. Every day would provide a new fight, my part was to stay ever ready.

Come and get me, I'll pluck an eye out or bite an ear off. In here I had to give a sign of mental sickness for people to leave me alone. There was not too much meat on my bones. Everyone else weighed over two hundred pounds. My only option was going to be maiming my attackers to prevent a future altercation.

There was nothing to do but stare at the ceiling four hours waiting for an answer. The other inmates had games, or worked out all day. They told the same story over and over about how they "Caught a case" like cops were throwing them out. I knew we all did something wrong and I was not apt on making friends.

Each block was assigned a time for the cafeteria, ours was last. The inmates complained about the food, one saying to me "Get ready for the leftovers." I was not sure what he meant until reaching the front of the line. The kitchen made enough food for the first three blocks. Anything left over from previous meals was then heated up for block D.

My selections were similar to that of a wine, age based. There was day old lasagna or a nice two day stroganoff. The oldest item there was rumored to be months old. It was a beet soup that had been frozen and reheated to a point where it changed colors to black. It looked like Ink soup, or food from the seventh layer of hell. I chose the lasagna but after one bite, lost my appetite and gave my food away. The inmate who took it was a skin head covered in tattoos. He gave me some advice "Hope you aren't in here long, if you are, then you need calories."

I was baffled by what that meant at the time, but I hoped that someone would bail me out. Unfortunately it did not happen that night and it turned into an overnight. I fell asleep easily, it had been a long tiring day. One of the worst and most confusing days of my life actually. I can see why I drifted off so easily, my mind wandered to dreaming about Christy. In my head I was with her back home, watching movies on the couch. My dad walked into the room in full health. Then falling deeper, my father had on boxing gloves. He was teaching me how to fight.

"Brian, what's the first rule of boxing?" My father asked in the dream.

Suddenly I was a young child with gloves on as well. Learning to fight at the age of six or seven. I answered my father.

"Protect yourself at all times!" My child voice shouted.

Then I awoke realizing I was in danger. My body was trying to warn me, or my dad's spirit. Something let me know that my guard was down and in trouble. It was too late, five men pinned me down. Each holding a limb and one covering my mouth so I wouldn't scream for help.

"You're on the inside now pretty boy, I need a new bitch."

I fought and flinched with all my might, my stiches tore open struggling for freedom. It was terrifying to know how helpless I truly was. These men overpowered me in seconds. Who knows what they were going to do, I was too weak for raw strength. Still I resisted and tried to call for help. A guard heard the commotion and shined his light over.

"Hey! What's going on over there? Get back to your bunks now!"

The men released me and walked back to their beds.

"See you tomorrow stud." One of them said squeezing his lips together to make a kissing noise.

Thank God an honest guard was on duty, it was truly divine intervention. I was helpless against these animals and I called for help. Destitute for aid I called on God under my breath and he answered me. There wasn't another attempt that night.

Before lunch the next day I was informed my bail was posted. This was unheard of for inmates in block D. Normally their bail was too high to pay, most were comfortable where there were. They got used to a life of normalcy behind bars. I stared down one of my attackers from the previous night. We exchange no further words.

Leaving the jail I expected to see Vince and Christy waiting for me. It was only Tanner alone holding a bag full of cheeseburgers from a fast food place.

"Hey bud!" I gave him a big hug, thanked him for bailing me out.

"Here! You have to be hungry B. I know the kind of food they have in there." Tanner gave me the bag of food.

"Thank you, you're right I'm starving."

"Come on kid, let's get you back so you can shower."

"Are you saying I stink?"

"Yes."

I laughed. "Hey do you know a ghetto doctor?"

"Of course, why?" He asked concerned.

I showed Tanner my loose stiches.

"Ewe bro! That's gross, okay yeah I'll call one after your shower." He said.

"Is Vince and Christy at the house?"

Tanner lit a cigarette and handed me one as well.

"After eight-ball and the hospital the state took the kids. I tried to take them in, but couldn't get custody. So I got ahold of your grandpa Christy. He has them in Kansas now."

I was deeply saddened by the news, but relieved they weren't in foster care. I just wanted to hold onto my family and kiss my sister on the head. We had been through so much together, I needed them by my side.

Tanner said that Vince left him the money he saved. That's how I was bailed out of jail. Tanner told me that I'd need every penny of it to fight the case. He said that the best thing to do was to push the self-defense plea. The District Attorney had a real hard-on for the case and wanted to see me do hard time. He wanted to make an example out of me and lock me away forever.

Tanner told me that Angel left her number so she can stay in the loop. Ashley called, so Tanner told her my situation, afterwards she offered to pay part of the bail. I had friends when I needed them, the block had my back.

After getting cleaned up, a doctor came over to sew me back together. He had this long story about how he lost his practice of his "Bitch of a wife." He lost everything in the divorce. Most of what he makes goes to alimony, thus he operates underground. I loved it, the thought of a shade-tree Doctor astonished me. He patched me up and went on his merry way, very easy.

Tanner's house felt lonely without my siblings. Spanish was gone and Lance went missing. It was just me and Tanner, half his crew had been wiped out. Fight night was surly dead as well. We sat in his living room in silence sipping beer before he spoke to me.

"How was it on the inside? Did you learn anything?"

"Yeah, the food sucks and something about needing calories."

"Calories? Who said that? Or what did they say?"

"A bigger guy who I gave my lunch to said it."

"Oh, I see. Yeah he means you're too skinny for jail. Most guys your size get turned into bitches."

"Yeah⋯" I put my head down, reluctant to tell him about the attack. He knew that something was up though.

"Oh shit, did something happen Brian? Do you want the neighborhood shrink?"

"Alright, calm down wise guy, nothing happened. But it got dangerously close."

"And how did that make you feel?"

"Helpless." Tanner was patronizing me but I still replied. He became sympathetic when my mood remained the same.

"Hey don't feel bad kid, we are at an advantage this time."

"How so Tanner?"

"On the inside you either have to be big or psycho. It's easier out here to beef you up. I can monitor your diet and get you there quick."

"You think I am going back?"

"Honestly I have no idea, but wouldn't you rather be prepared? We can push the hearing off for months."

"You're making a lot of sense."

"If it were me Brian, I would be eating right this second. You're what? One-eighty-five sopping wet? You need to put on thirty pounds at least."

"Are you serious? There's no way I can gain that much weight!"

"Trust me B, we can get you there. I know a ghetto trainer who you can work with."

"Any other options?"

"Mexico." Tanner said sarcastically, but it was an option.

Going on the run for the rest of my life sounded ridiculous. I was tired of running. It was time for me to finally answer for my sins, at least I could go comfortable. I agreed to have Tanners guy train me, he was thrilled. He made a phone call and told me Daniel a former inmate would be over in the morning to start my training.

We jumped right in, he was at Tanners house at six in the morning the next day. He was in his fifty's or sixties but had slabs of muscle. He had been incarcerated for twenty years of his life and he was the perfect person to train me. He could teach me about life on the inside and surviving.

"Get up punk! Time to move sucka!" an elder man with light brown skin and white hair yelled in my face.

"Hi, my name is Brian. Can I brush my teeth first?"

"The name is Daniel punk! Get your pasty ass out of bed and up the damn stairs!"

"Yes sir!" I sprung out of bed and hustled up the stairs to start his lessons.

"Okay, listen up boy. You are on my time now, just like the inside. Now you are going to do three things when we are together. That's eat, lift and read. You can sleep and shit in your own time, unless you want the full experience."

I shook my head back and forth for a definite no, not knowing he was joking. He continued.

"Now I'm only going to be with you for two weeks, after that you can apply yourself on your own. Just follow what I say and you'll be okay if you go in, agree?"

"Yes." I said eagerly. Maybe I could put on thirty pounds of muscle. If anyone could show me how it was this guy.

"Okay then let's start now. Time to eat."

We went to the kitchen where he made me breakfast. The portion size was tremendous, but very simple. A plate full of scrambled eggs and a bowl full of oatmeal. I looked at the size of the meal and doubted I could eat the whole thing.

"How many eggs is this?"

"Infinity mother fucker! Just eat the shit! I don't want to see a single bite left."

It was crazy how often this guy yelled, he was truly giving me the complete experience. I didn't want nothing to do with him, but needed to prepare for worst case scenario.

Just like Daniel said I ate every bite and then wanted to throw-up by how full I was. But he didn't let me rest, it was straight to work. His routines were basic but obvious. After the first day of training I knew that he was preparing for prison by the hour.

We ate breakfast early in the morning when it would be served in lock-up. I read during block hours. He made me read " *The art of war*" and classic literature. He said that there are few "Dumb mother fuckers" in prison. They knew things that would astonish me.

He had me eat three big meals a day. Those meals mimicked cafeteria food, fill up the plate to gain mass. He said I needed three times the amount of calories I currently ate to gain mass. Then we had to work off the excess to stay burning and building. Every workout was to failure. Push-up to failure, pull-ups... If I was too weak to do a single rep then we moved on to squats and variations of it. After an hour of working out in place, I grew rather hungry.

"Back to the cell for carbs." Daniel said jokingly. He lightened up when he knew I followed orders.

Carbs that he fed me on cell block hour were not healthy. It consisted of foods that could be purchased from commissary on the inside with money on my account. He fed me two packages of dried noodles with chips crushed on top for flavor. The snack was actually quite tasty, then he had me run for miles.

I would have rather ran for miles down the road but Daniel had a different plan. He had me run around the block for a solid hour. The same circle over and over, he did this to mimic the track I could run on in prison. It scared me knowing I might be going away for years. That fear kept me going through the training for a solid two weeks straight. The routine was the same every day. From six in the morning till eight o' clock in the evening.

Just like he said, eat, train and read. That is all that we did. I learned to shower before he arrived and after he left so it was on my time. Bathroom breaks could be used during meal time if I ate fast enough. The routine sounded crazy but after two weeks of training I had gained fifteen pounds. He left me to train the next several months without him. Just like a cool breeze in the summer time he vanished into thin air almost.

After seeing the results, I kept with the training and exact regimen without him. There was nothing else to focus on, my family was away for their own safety and I was preparing for the next chapter in my life. A new fight, a new ghetto and a bigger landscape for trouble. Tanner would not be with me and could not help me more than he did.

The next few months flew by faster than I expected. Every night I prayed for my family and looked forward to the next day of training. Tanner opened up a second grow operation, he needed the extra income without fight night he tried to keep me focused by sparing each day together. I was dedicated and determined to keep my agenda no matter the outcome.

I was eating a dozen eggs with a bowl of grits and a bowl of oatmeal. I reached over a hundred pull-ups in succession before failure. Kicks were incorporated into my shadow boxing and sparing with Tanner. It felt like I was becoming an assassin, every bone in my body was trained to the maximum.

The day of my trial came and mentally I was prepared. The courtroom was no longer scary. My fear of the results were no longer an issue. Whatever happens, happens. If it was meant for me to be alone for years on end then so be it. Maybe God's plan was for me to pay for everything that happened.

Tanner wore a suit to my hearing and I wore a long sleeve shirt tucked into jeans. Most of my clothes were too tight and even what I was wearing was uncomfortable. We sat in the courthouse waiting for our case to be called. Tanner and I arrived early that day.

"Tanner!" Christy yelled from down the hall.

Vince and she ran to greet him, not recognizing me.

"Holy crap! Brian?" Vince ran and hugged me.

"Brian!" Christy ran to my side.

"Wow, how did you gain so much muscle. Are you doing steroids?" Vince asked.

"Of course not, otherwise I'd have a six-pack." I laughed messing with Vince. "I've missed you both so much, can't believe you are here. How did you get here?"

My siblings turned to two men at the end of the hall. My father and my grandpa Christy.

Eli had come out of the comma a few weeks prior. He was able to walk, but needed a cane for assistance. My grandfather Christy must have just given back custody. I rushed to my father's side to greet him.

"Dad! You're up! Not the best of circumstances, but I've missed you. So much has happened."

"Son, I'm here now, I'm so sorry you went through everything."

"Good morning to you Brian." My grandfather said. I hugged him as well.

"Hey grandpa."

"How've you been lad?"

"I've been better."

"True, not the best of circumstances us being here. Lot of naysayers and willie wishers." He responded in a thick Irish accent.

"Not sure what that means, but you're right."

"Son, how did you get so big? Have I been gone that long?"

"Yes dad you have, I just eat and train all day to prepare for this."

"Wow, well lord willing you won't do any real time." Eli said.

"Yeah I hope so, but I'd rather be safe you know?"

"Suppose you're right." He said.

"What's the first rule of boxing?" I asked my father.

"Protect yourself at all times." He smiled knowing I took life lessons from him.

"Brian Vega, case two-two-seven!" A woman called for me to go on trial.

The case lasted a few hours, I expected the trial to go on for months. After all the facts had been presented and testimonies read, it was pretty much over. We had an intermission for a quick decision and that was it.

The judge was in her fifties with a real distaste for me. I was sentenced five to seven years hard time in Kansas state penitentiary. She only gave me forty eight hours to say my goodbyes and get my affairs in order. After that I had to turn myself over to serve the sentence for involuntary manslaughter.

My family cried for me, I was ashamed at what I've become. The consequences of my actions would haunt me for the rest of my life. I didn't want my brother to follow down the same path, those were my mistakes. My family deserved better, I did what I had to, to protect them, and I just crossed the line in the end.

Tanner was going to stay up the entire night collecting information to help me on the inside. Where I was going, what block they had me in, he knew someone who could get all of that info.

They only gave me two days, so the first day I went back home with my family. The ride home felt like a family road trip, all we were missing was mom. It was like we were children again, on the way to visit grandpa slick.

My siblings made me forget that I was going to prison. We shared laughs and old stories the entire drive home. Grandpa Christy sat in the front with my father. Grandma was still in Ireland, but he came when he heard we were in trouble. Funny how it worked out like that. My grandfather could have been our saving grace from the start. I thought the same thing at the time, but chose the wrong grandparent to pursue.

Grandpa Christie would put his life on the line to protect his grandchildren. He was strict, but he loved us and wanted the best. Who knows where my story would be if I had just called him. What if I never pushed that nice officer? He was doing his job. If I let Tanner fend for himself the day I met him, where would we be? Still on the streets? There were too many regrets in my heart, it was too late for that. I couldn't feel sorry for myself. I had to just enjoy the moment and look to the end of the tunnel. When I came out I would be twenty-three to twenty-five years old. In my head, life was over after that. There would be no college, marriage, kids, home or family. Just loneliness living in seclusion on the opposite ends of the law.

Most people who get out of prison go back, life changes so much while you're gone. It's hard to cope with the ever changing environment. Some people probably get caught on purpose to go back to a life that they understand. This became my greatest fear, I did not want this one decision to define my life. There had to be a greater cause, something that I could take away from the situation.

My thoughts were kept to myself, my family deserved only smiles. Grandpa Christy told us stories about mom when she was young. It made my father uncomfortable for some reason, like he did not want us knowing that side of her.

He said that Alice was a rebel, she smoked and got a tattoo on her buttock of a smiley face. Just for pure rebellion, she was a girl who lived in the now. He went on to talk about how she was friends with uncle Vinny first. Then my father interrupted him and changed subjects. Was my mother part of something I didn't know about? I never saw her "Rebel" side. Either was I knew one day grandpa Christie would spill the details of my mother, I'd just have to ask him when my father isn't here.

We ate pizza that night just like every weekend growing-up. Dad knew it was my favorite and there was a new pizzeria that had opened next to the old house. The pizza was alright at best compared to Luigi's. Eli rented war movies that grandpa and he agreed upon. The night faded before my eyes, I cherished each passing moment. Vince started learning the guitar from living with grandpa. He had an old acoustic he loved to play now and again. Vince picked up on his lessons with ease, he was a natural musician. Grandpa let Christy pick an after school project, she chose dance. She loved every class, it gave her an outlet to express herself without words. Perfect for a gentle soul.

My dad was mainly focusing on rehab for his legs after months of not using them. He wrote in his free time, telling me he was working on something big. My grandfather Christy was happy to spend time with the kids and treated them as guests. We would have been well taken care of living with him. He had to say farewell just before nightfall, catching his flight back to the old country.

Dad fell asleep on the couch to a movie and Christy laid near his feet. Vince and I talked about life after I did my time. He joked at the notion of being my boss if he went to college. The next half a decade would be hard. I could not be the older brother that I wanted to be. His role model had fallen from the life of the fabulous. I told him that his true talent would be in designing a game rather than playing them. He could probably see all the bugs and make something more fun.

He loved the idea but told me that he wanted to become an architect instead. Vince loved drawing but was embarrassed that he could not draw characters very well. He loved drafting and architecture because it was all lines and shapes. It was very methodical and easy to comprehend. Creating a structure from simple shapes. Vince said when he becomes famous I can be his body guard.

"You got freaking massive Brian."

"That was the intention Vince."

"Why? You want to be a meathead?"

"What would you do if you were in my shoes Vince?"

"Good point."

"How's Tanner doing? Any new project?" He asked me.

"Nothing exciting, he misses you guys like I do."

"Yeah we miss him too, he gave me his number after your arrest. I just didn't want to bother him."

"Well, I don't think it would hurt to check in now and then. Especially when I'm gone."

"Think so?"

"Hell yeah bro, it would probably make his day to hear from you. He watched us like family, you know?"

"Yeah, guess so. Hey Brian, can I write you while you serve time?"

"Please do, it will be lonely in there. You don't have to visit every week or nothing though. That would make it harder, seeing you come and go. Meanwhile I am in a cage."

"When should we come to see you then?"

"Come when you absolutely need to see me in person. Otherwise save something for the letters and know I'm with you in my heart."

"Why do you have to go Brian? It's not fair." He said fighting the urge to weep.

"Hey buddy, I'll be out before you know it. Just be stronger for me okay?"

"Okay, but don't come out any bigger or you will be an actual Ox."

"No promises there bro." We laughed and joked around until there was a light knock at the door. I went to investigate.

"Hey, is Brian here?" Angel asked then in a second glance said. "Holy shit! Brian what have you been eating? You're massive!"

"Everything, I've been eating literally everything. Come in!"

My family was happy to see her, dad and Christy woke up from their nap. She joined in playing midnight board games and just spending time together. Everyone seemed to be fighting sleep at my expense. So I insisted that everyone rest up. They had to drive me back the next day to meet up with Tanner. He was going to take me the rest of the way, straight to prison. Everyone but Angel and I went to bed. We stayed up the whole night, not sleeping for a moment. She told me that she still loved me and would never stop. Even while I was away. It might have been a lie, but I needed to hear it. We made love that night and snuggled till sunrise, thinking about the future. The next morning she said goodbye and told me that she would write me every week. I'll believe it when I see it, but it was a good thought.

My father drove me to meet up with Tanner after I hugged and kissed my siblings goodbye. They stayed behind, it was too difficult to prolong saying farewell. My father drove in silence while my siblings held each other from a far. They will be missed.

We drove for hours without a word being spoken. He must have felt partially responsible for what happened. His eldest son was became a man by fighting off wolves. Eli knew that I would be fighting for my life every day. Always looking over my shoulder. He owed me some answers, I had to know what was going on.

"Dad why are there people trying to kill us?"

He looked at me for a moment contemplating an appropriate response.

"Son I used to be a different person, your mom was too. It's easy to get into a life that you are born into. Slick is responsible for that."

"What do you mean?"

"He held us like prisoners, Brian. Slick made us do things I never thought I could do, it's why I left that life. We were always being hunted, we were just protected."

"At what cost?"

"My brother, Vinny. He got me out not once but twice."

Tears rolled down his face thinking about uncle Vinny.

I accepted his answer with conviction. I would have to find answers for myself. We drove the rest of the way talking about mom and the crazy things that she used to do. She loved punk rock in the eighties and smoked in the girl's bathroom at school. She was suspended several times for fighting and cursed like a sailor. Her father used to say it was because of her Irish blood. Maybe that is where I got the criminal gene. I inherited her anger and the Irish will of fire, loving a good fight now and again. We came to a stop and my father welted up in tears.

"Son, I Love you, please stay safe. You will be in my prayers every night. Goodbye son." He hugged me before I opened the door to leave.

"Time to become a man."

"Son, that happened a long time ago." He waved goodbye.

I jumped into Tanners car and drove towards my eminent fate. He was eager to see me, he placed a folder on my lap filled with paper.

"What's this?"

"One last gift, Tech came through for me. He knew the Vega name. It turns out that your uncle is pretty well known in KC. He goes by a different name."

"Really? He was there all along?"

"Not quite, give those papers a quick once over. He was held in Missouri State Penitentiary in Jefferson City until two thousand and four. Then the prison closed down and he was moved."

"Holy shit, you went in depth."

"Guess where he was moved." Tanner exclaimed.

"Where?"

"Lansing Correctional, you are literally going to the same location."

"Seriously? Is he still there?"

"Yep, but it gets even better. He is known in Kansas City as Graveyard or the Grave Digger."

"That psycho guy who runs shit from prison?"

"One in the same, your uncle Vinny is the most feared man in KC."

"This is crazy Tanner, do you think he is well connected in there?"

"Are you kidding me? Did you not just hear what I said? You just hit the freaking lottery. Your time in there will be lush now, those years will fly by in minutes. You are going to a place where you are royalty."

"That's a bit of a stretch isn't it Tanner?"

"Not really, you are like a 'Lost Prince' coming home. He has to know you are coming by now."

"So now it's easy street?"

"Maybe, be on your guard B. Don't change that, but aren't you excited to know him better?"

"Yeah, you're right. I'm more nervous than anything."

"Don't be, it is going to be the hardest thing you will ever do. But if anyone could do it, it's you. With or without your psycho uncle."

The ride to Lansing was short, it only took about twenty minutes from where Tanner had picked me up. We arrived at the gate of the prison just before two in the afternoon, I unloaded my few belongings and said my peace in place of a farewell. After all it was not goodbye for good. There were still many unwritten chapters in my life. I was going to find out who was pursuing us and why dad left. Lock-up would be hard, it was good to know someone from the start. I held my head high, it was time to pay the price for my actions. God help me.

End of Vol.1

www.ingramcontent.com/pod-product-compliance
Lightning Source LLC
Chambersburg PA
CBHW061610170626
46811CB00001B/378